Getting to Know Your Pony

Getting to Know Your Pony

Sandy Ransford

© Stabenfeldt AS
Getting to Know Your Pony
© Text: Sandy Ransford
The Ronald Duncan Literary Foundation has granted permission to
include the horse poem A Tribute to the Horse.
© Cover photo: Bob Langrish.
Cover horse: Miniature Wee Bucking Willy
© Photos: Page 56, 73, 90, 91, 92, 94, 96, 97, 99, 100, 101, 102, 104,
105, 106, 114, 115, 117, 119, 121, 123, 129, 130, 131, 137 and 138:
Marielle Andersson Gueye. Photos of fly fringe page 89 and girth page
117 from Hööks Hästsport.
All other photos © Bob Langrish.
© Illustrations: Jennifer Bell.
Layout: Stabenfeldt AS
Editor: Bobbie Chase
Printed in Italy.
Published by Pony 2008.

ISBN: 1-933343-73-7

Stabenfeldt, Inc.
457 North Main Street
Danbury, CT 06811
www.pony.us

Contents

This book is dedicated to horses and ponies throughout the world, and to everyone who treats them kindly.

6

A Tribute to the Horse

Where in this wide world can man find nobility without pride,
friendship without envy or beauty without vanity?
Here, where grace is laced with muscle, and strength by gentleness confined.

He serves without servility; he has fought without enmity.
There is nothing so powerful, nothing less violent;
there is nothing so quick, nothing more patient.

England's past has been borne on his back.
All our history is his industry,
We are his heirs, he our inheritance.
Ladies and gentlemen –
The Horse.

Ronald Duncan

This poem was written for Britain's
internationally famous Horse of the Year
Show in 1954. It makes us realize what
wonderful animals horses are, and how
lucky we are that they let us ride them.

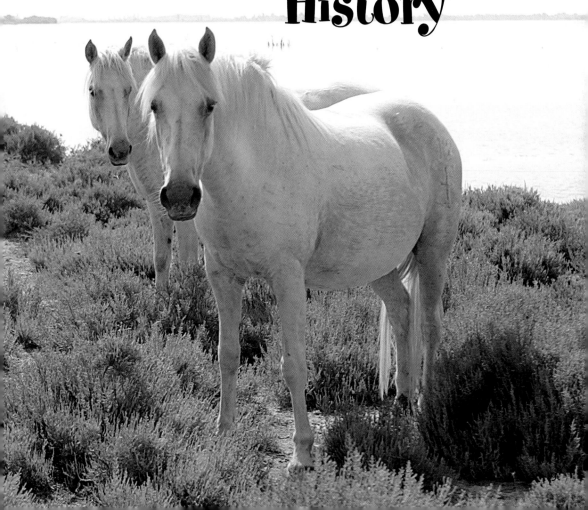

A Pony's History

A Pony's History

Way Back in the Past

History? If this sounds too much like school, just hang in a minute. We all have history. We all have ancestors who lived hundreds and even thousands of years ago, and ponies are no exception. Knowing a bit about how modern ponies came into being helps us to understand more about them. So prepare to be amazed!

Although there are now many different breeds and types of horses and ponies, they are all descended from the same ancestors. The earliest ones we know of lived about 60 million years ago in North America. That's an awfully long time ago! Scientists call this forerunner of today's horses and ponies Eohippus, or the "dawn horse." It didn't look much like today's animals. For a start it was tiny, about the size of a fox. It didn't have hooves, either. On its front feet it had four toes, like a cat or dog; on its hind feet it had three toes. Its tail looked like a cow's, with a tuft of hair at the end, and it grazed on trees and other plants rather than on grass.

Gradually, over millions of years, this little animal changed to become more like the equines we know today. This

Eohippus – the Dawn Horse

change is called evolution. It grew taller, and its toes gradually became fewer, until it ended up with a single toe on each leg, the hoof. The little growths on the insides of a pony's legs, which we call "chestnuts," are believed to be the remnants of one of its toes. Its teeth changed, too, and adapted to grazing plants on the ground rather than browsing off branches. Its neck became longer, and the position of its eyes became higher and more to the side of its head, like those of the modern horse or pony, so it can see to the side and behind it as well as to the front. Its tail became the long switch of hairs that it is today. And so, a mere one million years ago, the first form of the modern horse and pony, called by scientists Equus caballus, came into being.

During the Ice Ages, when ice sheets and glaciers covered the world, Equus caballus moved from North America to Europe and Asia. Around 10,000 years ago, equines became extinct in North America, and none existed there from that time until the Spanish conquistadors took horses there in the 16th century. These Spanish horses became the ancestors of the American breeds, including the wild herds that roamed the West, called mustangs.

Equus caballus

Development of Horses and Ponies in Europe and Asia

Those early horses that moved to Europe and Asia during the Ice Ages developed into four primitive types, from which the breeds we know today have descended.

1. In Mongolia, one developed into Przewalski's Horse. This pony-sized animal is a typical "primitive horse." It is dun colored, with a dorsal stripe like the Highland and Fjord ponies, and has an upright mane and a large, heavy head. These ponies still exist, and can be seen in zoos and nature preserves.

2. West of the Caspian Sea was the tarpan, a slim, lightly built creature, which had a dun coat that turned white in winter. The tarpan is technically extinct, but scientists bred a modern animal from ponies that were typical examples, and there is a herd of "tarpans" in Poland today.

3. In northern Scandinavia there was the Forest Horse. This is now extinct, but it was thought to be a heavy, thick-legged, large-footed browsing animal, which became an ancestor of the European heavy horse breeds.

4. The fourth primitive type existed in Siberia and was called the Tundra Horse. It is also extinct nowadays, but in Siberia there are white-coated ponies called Yakut that may be its descendants.

Przewalski horses

Przewalski
Horse

Getting a Bit More Up to Date

We get nearer to modern horses and ponies with discoveries scientists made in the 20th century. They studied early equine bones and teeth, and came to the conclusion that four further types existed in Europe and Asia approximately 5000 to 6000 years ago.

Pony Type 1

was around 12.2 hands high and lived in northwest Europe. It could survive in cold, wet conditions, with poor grazing. It had some similarities to Britain's Exmoor pony.

Pony Type 2

was larger, around 14.2 hands high, and lived in Asia. It was similar to Przewalski's Horse, and could withstand very cold conditions. Britain's Highland Pony resembles it in some ways.

Horse Type 3

came from eastern Asia. It was around 14.3 hands high, lightly built and thin-skinned, with a long body, and able to tolerate hot conditions. It was believed to be similar to today's Akhal Teke breed.

Horse Type 4

came from western Asia. Although it was called a horse, it was only 10 – 11 hands high. It was lightly built, with a high-set tail, a "dished" (concave in profile) face, and was also able to tolerate heat. It is believed to be a forebear of the Caspian Pony, which, in turn, may be an ancestor of the Arab.

Exmoor
Ponies

16

Highland
Ponies

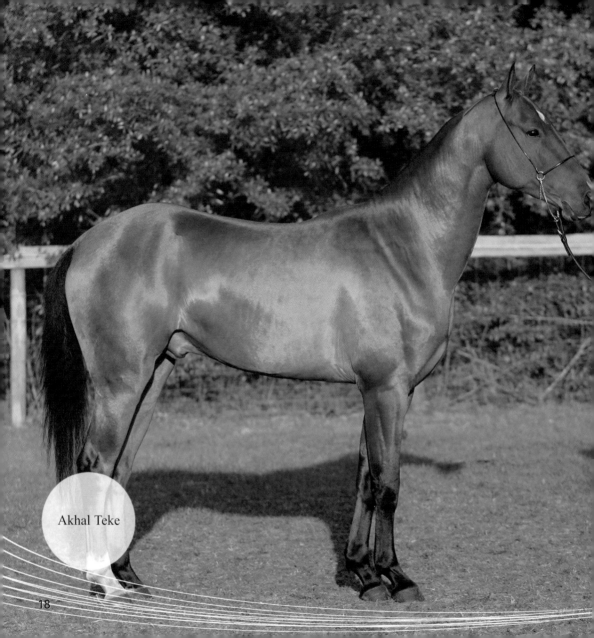

Akhal Teke

Caspian
Pony

And Then What?

Over thousands of years, these types of horses and ponies developed and evolved. The way this happened was partly due to genetic influences, and partly a result of the environment in which they lived. The size of an animal, for example, is very much influenced by its environment. In northern Europe, where there is heavy rainfall that produces plenty of lush grazing, horses grew to be large and heavy, and developed into heavy work horses such as the Dutch Draft, the Shire, the Jutland, the Brabant and the Ardennais. In high, wild mountain and moorland areas, where food was poor, the climate harsh and the terrain rough, small, hardy, sure-footed ponies thrived, which became breeds like the Dartmoor and Exmoor of Britain, and the Icelandic.

Icelandic Horses

Shire

Dartmoor Pony

Desert areas, where food was scarce and the temperature changed from great heat in the daytime to freezing cold at night, produced light, swift horses of enormous stamina, like the Arab. These sorts of horses, which were purebred for many generations, are called "hotbloods." They originally came from the Middle East and North Africa, and the breeds include the Arab, the Barb, the Caspian, and horses bred from them, like the English Thoroughbred.

The heavy horses from northern Europe are known as "coldbloods."

Those breeds in between are called "warmbloods," and were originally bred by crossing hotbloods and coldbloods. They combine the speed and "rideability" of the hotbloods with the calmer temperament of the coldbloods. Many of today's most successful competition horses (i.e. eventers, dressage horses, show-jumpers) such as the Hanoverian, Dutch Warmblood, Trakehner and Holstein, are warmbloods. Just to make life even more confusing, most pony breeds are not classified in this way! Many pony breeds have existed for

Arabian

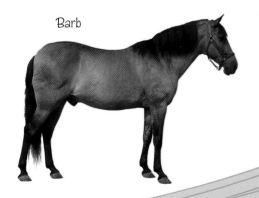

Barb

hundreds, and even thousands, of years.

All clear now? The only problem is, most of the horses and ponies you will meet will not be purebred. And, in addition, there are "types" of horses and ponies. So, what's the difference between a breed and a type?

Trakehner

Hanoverian

Dutch Warmblood

Breeds and Types

Although not many horses and ponies are purebred, most fall into some kind of "type." This might be a riding pony type (one that is suitable for children to ride), a hunter type (one that can gallop across country and jump), cob type (a short, stocky animal capable of carrying a heavy rider), and so on.

A breed was originally a group of horses or ponies that lived in a specific area, and was influenced by local conditions such as food availability and climate. Because they were all subject to the same influences, and they interbred, they tended to be similar in size, shape, color, height and action. As humans stepped in and began to want horses for specific purposes, they bred them specially for those purposes, and a breed became established.

For example, if breeders wanted to produce very fast horses, they would breed from the fastest mare and the fastest stallion they had, to try and produce an even faster horse. They could

Cob type

Riding Pony

also breed out defects, such as weak joints or poor feet, by not breeding from horses and ponies that had these faults. In this way, they produced particular breeds of horses and ponies for specific purposes, such as racing, pulling a plough, pulling a heavy coach or a light, fast carriage, being a quiet and reliable riding horse, or fighting with the cavalry. That is why today we have so many different breeds and types of horses and ponies.

Ancient breeds like the Arab, the Barb and some of the pony breeds are "natural" breeds, because they existed and were of a similar type before humans started breeding them. In modern times, the names and pedigrees of all purebred horses and ponies are entered in a stud book, and only those animals whose parents' names are in the stud book are considered purebred.

What's the Difference Between a Horse and a Pony?

Ponies stand up to 14.2 hands high (58 inches). Horses are 14.3 hands high (59 inches) and taller. A "hand" is the traditional way of measuring the height of a horse or pony, and it is 4 inches or 10 cm, and was meant to be the width of a man's hand. Nowadays, horses and ponies are also measured in inches. There are other differences apart from height. Ponies have shorter legs and smaller ears than horses. They are deeper through the body, and stronger, in relation to their size. They are usually sure-footed and tend to have strong characters. They can be willful and quite naughty! The native pony breeds are very hardy, able to withstand the winter weather, and live very well on comparatively small amounts of not very good food. If they are fed large amounts of hard feed or lush grass, they are likely to get laminitis, a painful inflammation of the feet.

But let's go back a bit and see how the relationship between people and ponies first started.

When People First Met Ponies

Unfortunately, for those of us who love ponies, scholars who have studied ancient history believe that humans' first contact with equines was to hunt them for food. About 6,000 years ago, instead of just stalking and hunting herds of wild ponies, they began to herd them together – a sort of early farming of horses, in the way people keep sheep nowadays. It is also just possible that these early humans may have tried to ride their horses. Most records show that horses and ponies were driven before they were ridden. They pulled chariots that were used for racing, for hunting wild animals, and in battles. But scientists who have studied fossilized remains

Pony

Horse

of horses' teeth have found grooves on them that they think may have been made by bits in the horses' mouths. And they think that these fossils are at least 500 years older than the invention of the wheel. This is believed to date back to 3,500 BC, when wheeled vehicles were used in Sumeria, a country that existed approximately where modern Iraq is. So if the horses weren't being used for driv-ing, it is likely that they were being rid-den. We can only wonder what made a human being so many years ago first climb onto the back of a horse. Those early humans must have been very brave and adventurous!

Whether driving or riding came first, we do know that for centuries people drove chariots using horses. The Romans, in particular, are famous for their chariot races, which took place in arenas such as the Circus Maximus in Rome. Great and bloody battles were also fought from chariots. But these early vehicles were unwieldy. They were not easy to turn quickly, because they had to be driven around in a large semi-circle to turn or they would tip over. So, although they could move fast in a straight line, they were not easy to maneuver. At some stage someone must have realized that ridden horses were much more maneuverable than driven ones, and could also move faster, so cavalry began to replace the chariots for war.

People began to use horses for other purposes, too. The light, fast horses may have been used by the cavalry, but the stronger, heavier ones were useful on the farms, to pull ploughs and heavy loads. For centuries, until the early 20th century, horses and ponies spent their lives in the service of people, many of them working extremely hard. Nowadays we use them mostly for fun. Most of these animals, whether in the past or today, live lives that are far removed from those of their early ancestors. So what is a pony's natural life like? How would it live if it were not under the control of human beings?

A Pony's Natural Life

29

A Pony's Natural Life

Family Life

There aren't many truly wild horses and ponies left in the world today, but the semi-wild ones live in much the same way as their ancestors would have done. They live in family groups. These consist of a stallion, a group of mares and their foals, plus a few young animals that stay around the family group until they are old enough to leave and form other groups, or herds, of their own. Within the group, one horse, usually a senior mare, is the boss. It is she who decides where the ponies will graze, when

they will move on to another patch, when they will seek out drinking water, and so on. If other individuals challenge her authority by refusing to do what she wants, or by being a bit slow in obeying her, she soon puts them in their place. At the worst, this may mean she bites or kicks them, but more often she just lays back her ears, stretches her head forward

Exmoor Ponies playing in Exmoor, England

Semi-wild
Giara Ponies
on Sardinia,
Italy

toward the other horse and maybe bares her teeth, and this is enough to tell them that she is the boss, and that if they don't do as she wants, they must face the consequences.

Within the group ponies have their friends and their enemies. A group of domesticated horses and ponies is just the same today. Friends graze close to each other, moving on side by side. Sometimes they will stop grazing and groom each other, scratching at each other's necks or withers with their teeth. In hot summer weather they will stand nose to tail, dozing, keeping the flies off each other's faces by swishing their tails.

Exmoor Ponies resting in Exmoor, England

Enemies approach each other with their ears laid back and may bare their teeth. Sometimes they snap at their enemies, or even bite them hard. They may swing their quarters around ready to kick, or may actually kick out. They don't usually hurt each other in these encounters. The action is more often a bluff, and one usually gives way and walks off before the hostility gets too serious.

There is also, within the group, a strict pecking order. Beneath the boss horse or pony there is a second in command, then a third, and so on, until we get down to the one who is the least important in the group. Those at the top of the pecking order get the best patch of grass to graze on, the best position to shelter from the weather, and so on, and they work down the list until the poor pony at the bottom

just gets what no one else wants. He or she is often bullied by the others, forced to give up their food, and often harassed and made to move on constantly. Horses and ponies are not very kind to their enemies! It is for this reason that when you feed hay to a group of animals in a field, you need to put out more piles of hay than there are ponies, so even if one is bullied, it can always move on to a pile that no one else is eating.

The stallion guards his family jealously against any rivals. Sometimes a young male will try to steal some of his mares. The stallion will then gallop around to send the newcomer packing and, if this doesn't work, may challenge him by rearing up and striking out with his forelegs. He may also bite and kick. Again, the rival usually retreats before much harm is done. But when a stallion gets old, one day a newcomer will drive

New Forest
Stallion
guarding his
herd.

him off and take over the herd. In this way, nature ensures that only the strongest and fittest animals breed, and this means that the foals produced will be as strong and healthy as possible.

In their natural lives, ponies spend most of their day grazing. They eat grass and other plants and flowers growing on the ground, such as dandelions and clover, and will also eat young leaves off certain trees. Domesticated ponies often eat hawthorn hedges, especially in spring when the leaves are young and fresh. When they are grazing, they eat a little at a time at one spot, then move slowly on, sniffing out the areas where the best grass is growing. Ponies may eat for as much as 20 hours out of the 24. This sounds like a lot, but grass is not very nourishing as a food, and they must eat a large amount to get the nutrients they need.

Every so often, they drink. Ponies tend to go for several hours without drinking, and then take a long drink. This may be because, when grazing the plains, they

New Forest mare and foal in New Forest, England

have to travel some distance to get water. And it is the opposite of what we are told about giving them water when they are domesticated. But, in the wild state, their small stomachs are not filled with hard-to-digest food, as they may be when they are kept stabled. If we give domesticated horses long drinks of water

Wild Brumbies
in Australia

it can wash the food out of their stomachs too quickly, and give them colic. But in the wild state they have small amounts of food almost constantly moving through their digestive tract, so there is less danger of this. Also, grass has a lot more water in it than hay or hard feed, so they take in some water along with their food.

Most of the time, ponies don't move very fast at all, but if danger threatens, then the whole herd will gallop off to safety at high speed. In their wild state ponies are preyed upon by creatures such as mountain lions and wolves, and their defense is to run, as fast as possible. Those that cannot run fast, such as the very young, the very old, and those that are ill, are the ones likely to be caught. Again, this is nature's way of ensuring that only the fittest animals can breed, so the foals are produced by the best parents.

From time to time the ponies rest. This is usually while they are standing. They will rest one hind leg, let their heads droop, and go to sleep. Because of ligaments that support its position, a pony can go to sleep standing up without falling over. Ponies seldom lie down for more than an hour or so. When they do so, they sometimes lie partly on their stomachs and partly on their sides, with their legs tucked under them, but if they are really tired they stretch flat out on their sides. While some ponies rest, others stand guard, looking out for danger. Horses in a group never all sleep or all lie down at the same time, and domesticated ponies behave in exactly the same way.

Camargue
Pony and friend
in Camargue,
France

From Birth to Old Age - a Pony's Life Cycle

A horse or pony mare carries her foal for just over 11 months. This means that in her natural life a mature mare is almost permanently in foal. Foals are born in spring, when the weather improves, the sun is getting warmer and the grass is getting rich. This gives the mare lots of nourishment so she can provide plenty of good milk to feed her foal. When the foal is born, the mare licks it to clean it and to encourage it to stand up. A healthy foal gets to its feet half an hour after being born. It is very wobbly on its long legs, and sometimes falls over again, but it soon manages to stagger about and find its way to its

Exmoor mare and foal

Exmoor foal
having a rest

mother's udder so it can take its first feed. This feed is very important to the foal, as it gives it antibodies that help protect it from disease as it grows up.

As soon as the foal can stand, it can follow its mother. The foal's long legs enable it to move fast and keep up with the rest of the herd. In the wild, this is very important, as an animal that gets separated from the herd becomes easy prey for wild beasts. Its speed enables it to survive.

At first a foal lives on its mother's milk, but when it is a few weeks old it starts to nibble at grass. By the time it is six months old, it is weaned, which means it no longer depends on its mother and can survive by finding its own food.

When it is one year old, the foal is called a yearling. It continues growing and maturing until it is five or six years old, and from then until the age of about 12 are its best years. Horses and ponies that compete usually achieve their best results during these years, though many have working lives long beyond this. Ponies are considered old in their late teens and twenties. They can live to around 25 to 30 years, and a few live even longer than this.

Welsh mare and foal

Eriskay mare
and foal in
Scotland,
UK.

Telling a Pony's Age By Its Teeth

People who know about ponies can tell their age by their teeth. A newborn foal has no teeth. The two central front incisors appear when the foal is about ten days old, and it has a full set of milk teeth at six to nine months. By the age of five or six years, the pony has a full set of permanent teeth. These consist of six incisors and 12 molars on each jaw. Male horses and ponies have two additional teeth on each jaw between the incisors and molars, called tushes. As the animal gets older, its teeth appear to be longer, as the gums recede, and the front teeth slope more when seen from the side.

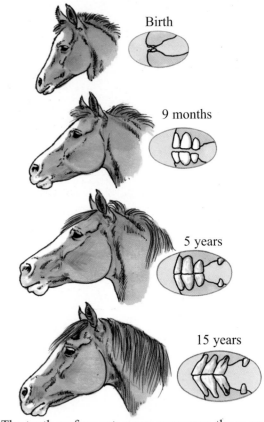

Birth

9 months

5 years

15 years

The tooth surface gets worn away over the years.

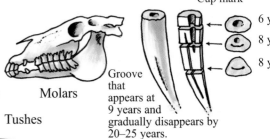

Cup mark

6 ye

8 ye

8 ye

Incisors

Molars

Tushes

Groove that appears at 9 years and gradually disappears by 20–25 years.

A Pony's Natural Life Compared With a Domesticated Pony's Life

When we keep a pony for riding, we make it live a very different life from that of its wild cousins. If it is stabled, it stands alone for long periods each day. It is fed rich food at regular intervals. For an hour or so a day, it may be worked hard and fast. This is all very different from its life of gently striding around, eating low quality food more or less all the time, surrounded by its friends. Even if it lives out in a field, it wanders around the same patch of ground all the time, whereas in the wild it would be constantly moving on to clean, fresh pastures.

To keep a pony happy and healthy, we need to try to mimic its natural life as much as possible. So we should feed it little and often, and give it lots of forage (that means grass, hay or haylage) to chew on to imitate grazing. If possible, we should keep it with other ponies, and put it out in a field with them for several hours each day to give it freedom to graze, to roam around, to roll, and to behave naturally. When we ride, we should start slowly and build up gradually to faster paces to give its muscles time to warm up – rather like an athlete preparing to run a race. All the time we are looking after, handling, and riding a pony, we need to think about its natural life, and try to recreate it as much as possible.

Friends are important!

A Pony's Senses

A Pony's Senses

A pony has the same five senses as you:
sight, hearing, taste, smell and touch.
But, on the whole, the pony's senses are
much more acute than yours are.

Sight

The prominent position of a pony's eyes
on either side of its forehead means it
can see almost 360 degrees. To the front,
both eyes together can see in a 65-
degree arc. This is called binocular
vision, and it enables the animal to
judge relative distances between objects
accurately. Each eye can see 146 degrees
to its own side and around to the back.
There is just a 3-degree gap immediately
behind the pony where neither eye can
see. And, strangely, when its head is
down, for example, when grazing, it
cannot see the grass it is cropping, nor
can it see a fence as it is actually jumping it. Instead, it has to rely on the image

it had of the jump a stride or two before it took off.

This almost all-around vision means that a pony can see most things that are going on around it. This is very useful in its wild state, as it can keep a good lookout for predators. Because ponies can see behind them as well as in front and to the side, driving horses and ponies have traditionally worn blinkers, to prevent them from seeing the vehicle behind them. Thinking that something was following close behind them would frighten many horses and ponies.

Whereas we see in color, scientists think that most animals, including ponies, cannot recognize colors in the same way as we do, and may see things more in terms of light and dark shades. Studies have shown that horses and ponies can tell red and blue from gray, but they cannot tell green from gray or white. It is thought that they see red, orange and yellow as more or less the same color. It is also possible that they see some colors more sharply than oth-

ers. Because of this, they seem to be affected by the contrast between light and shade more than we are. This could also be because their eyes take longer to adapt to lower levels of light than ours do. When you go from a brightly lit area to a dark one, your pupils dilate to allow more light to pass through your eye. Animals' eyes do this also, but it seems to take longer in horses and ponies. This may be one reason why so many dislike going from the light into dark places, such as a stable, horsebox or trailer, as to them it probably seems even darker than it really is.

When their eyes have adapted to the dark, they can see better in it than we can. We can make use of this if we have a pony that doesn't want to walk into a dark box or trailer. If you let it stand on the ramp, and cover its eyes with a thick scarf or a towel for a few moments, when you remove the cover it may well walk up the ramp quite happily. This is because, when you remove the scarf from its eyes, what it sees will be lighter

Like other animals (and even us, sometimes!), ponies tend to see things where they expect to see them. So if something is changed in their familiar surroundings, some may not notice. Others seem to notice something that is different immediately, and will stare at it, or, if they are very suspicious, snort at it.

than what it saw when its eyes were covered, so it will not perceive the box or trailer as being as dark as it was before.

Many ponies also dislike the color white. For example, they may refuse to walk past a patch of spilled white paint on the ground, or may stare at white markings on the road and possibly snort before walking past them. This could be because, to horses, white stands out very brightly against darker backgrounds, so they are suspicious of it.

Hearing

Animals, including ponies, have a much better sense of hearing than we do. They can hear a greater range of sounds (higher and lower) than we can, they can hear sounds that are not loud enough for us to hear at all, and they can place a sound accurately in space much better than we can. A pony can turn its ears outwards through 180 degrees from front to back, and each ear can move independently of the other. So when a pony hears a sound, it can turn either or both ears toward it, thus enabling it to hear the sound more clearly. If a pony finds an object interesting, it turns its ears toward it, even if the interesting object is emitting no sound.

Ponies enjoy hearing their owners' voices. If you speak to your pony when you are handling it, it helps to build a friendly relationship between the two of you. If you talk to your pony when you are riding, it will flick an ear back to listen to you, even if, with the other ear, it is concentrating on what is in front of it.

Horses and ponies learn very quickly to obey our spoken commands if we repeat the same words in the same tone of voice and accompany the words with the same actions. But it is very important to use the same tone of voice. The pony doesn't actually understand the words, but recognizes the tone. So if you say, "Good boy," in a warm, encouraging tone of voice, it will understand that you are praising it. If you shout the same words in an angry tone, it will think you are angry with it. So if you are disciplining it, you

need to say, "No!" very firmly, not in a vague sort of way. You should never shout or speak to a pony in anger, or it will be upset, and you may make it nervous and anxious. It can be difficult to remember this if you are excited or angry, but you must always try to speak to your pony in a quiet, reassuring tone, even if you have to be firm with it.

Smell

Ponies have a much more acute sense of smell than we do, and they use this sense to find out about things. Sniffing at the air gives them all kinds of information, in the same way as looking at something or listening tells us what is going on. If, for example, a strange person or animal approaches a pony, a

Two ponies meet and sniff

horse will be able to smell it, even if it cannot see them. A pony will sniff at your hands if you have been handling anything interesting, especially if it is some kind of food! And, although most ponies are greedy, if their food is musty, or if it has been contaminated, for example by mice, they will notice the scent and refuse to eat it.

All horses and ponies sniff at each other when they first meet. If they are unsure of each other, this can result in squeals and even swinging the hindquarters around ready to kick. When you meet a strange pony, it is a good idea to hold out your hand for it to sniff. But if you do this, keep your fingers curled up and offer it the back of your hand – just in case it takes a nip! Even when you are introducing a new piece of tack or equipment to a pony, it will appreciate you holding it up so it can take a sniff at it. This seems to be a way for the pony to assure itself that all is well.

When wild ponies are separated from their companions they seem to track them by sniffing at the piles of manure they leave behind. They stop and sniff at it, and the scent tells them which pony left which pile.

Sometimes it seems as if ponies use this connection between scent and manure to deliberately scent-mark their stables, as if claiming them for their own. It can be very annoying to put a pony in its beautifully clean stable, which you have laboriously mucked out, to find that it immediately manures or stales (urinates) in it!

Flehmen Reaction

Ponies, along with other animals, sometimes do an odd-looking thing with their top lips; they stretch them out and raise them, making a funny face as they do so. You may wonder what they are up to. This strange behavior is a way of enhancing the sense of

smell. It is called the Flehmen reaction, and a pony will often do it after it has sniffed at something it is suspicious of, or something it finds particularly interesting.

Taste

The senses of taste and smell are linked, and a pony's sense of taste is also very acute.

Unless it is starving, it will not eat food that doesn't taste as it should. Fields grazed by horses and ponies typically have patches of long, rank grass where the ponies leave piles of manure. These areas taste and smell sour, and the ponies will not eat the grass. Most ponies like a sweet taste – the taste of young, fresh grass and leaves, and of good hay. Some of the feeds we give, such as soaked sugar beet and molasses, also taste sweet, and most ponies find them

Taste good?

delicious. They are also very fond of sugar lumps! As is the case with humans, too much of these things are not good for a pony, but you can use them to your advantage sometimes. If your pony won't eat medicines such as wormers mixed in their feed, because they instantly know that it tastes wrong, they can often be persuaded to do so if the feed is smothered in molasses or soaked sugar beet to disguise the taste.

Sometimes ponies acquire a taste for bitter things, such as the weed tansy ragwort. Most ponies don't like the taste of this plant, but a few try it and then seem to get hooked on it, and will eat more and more if they get the chance. We have to stop them doing this, because the plant is very poisonous. Over a period of time it destroys the pony's liver. The more they eat, the worse the damage is, and ultimately it will kill them.

Touch

A pony can feel things through its skin just like you, but, unlike yours, its skin contains little muscles that it can contract. So, for example, when a fly lands on its body, it can twitch a muscle in exactly the right place to dislodge the fly.

A pony's whiskers are also part of its feeling mechanism. It has long whiskers on its muzzle and around its eyes, which it uses to feel its way around. They act like a cat's whiskers – they tell a pony what is near its face if it cannot see it. For example, as we saw in the section on sight, a pony cannot see what is on the ground where it is eating, but it can feel objects with its whiskers. For this reason, you should never trim a pony's whiskers. People used to do so, when preparing them for a show, in the belief that it made them look tidier, but if you do this, you are depriving them of part of their sense of touch, which is an unkind thing to do.

Some areas of the pony's skin are more sensitive to touch than others. Generally, the underparts of its body are more sensitive than the upper. So while it may not mind you scrubbing away at muddy patches on its back with a dandy brush, it may not be pleased if you try to give the same treatment to its tummy or between its back legs. The withers (at the base of the neck) are very sensitive, and it is here that ponies often nibble at each other, which clearly gives them pleasure. Most ponies enjoy humans scratching at their withers, too, and doing this can often calm down an anxious or nervous pony. But if a numnah presses down on the withers when you are riding, it will be uncomfortable for the pony.

The mouth is very sensitive to touch, and to pain – something you need to remember when riding a pony.

Sometimes riding school ponies seem to have mouths that don't feel anything, because they have been spoiled by lots of beginners riding them, but if you ride

Most ponies enjoy having humans scratch their withers

a well-schooled pony that has not been spoiled in this way you will find its mouth responds to the lightest touch. In this case, a light hand on the rein is much more comfortable for the pony.

We rely on ponies' sense of touch when we ride them, for the aids we give, through our hands, seat and legs, are felt by the pony through its sense of touch. And some ponies need stronger aids than others. A sensitive, thin-skinned animal will respond to your lightest touch; a tougher one, especially one that is used to beginners flapping their legs around, may need much more powerful aids. A young pony may take some time to respond to our touches, because at first it doesn't know what we want, but as it becomes better schooled and more experienced, it reacts to lighter touches.

Top Lip

A pony's top lip is also extremely sensitive, and it uses it to feel its way around, much in the same way an elephant uses its trunk – in fact, the top lip is a bit like a shortened version of an elephant's trunk. If you watch a pony grazing you can see it moving its top lip as it feels its way around the vegetation. If you give a pony a bowl of feed, for example chaff, with a few pony nuts or slices of carrot mixed in it, it will use its top lip to separate the tasty bits from the rest so it can eat them first.

Because the top lip is so sensitive, people used to use a device called a twitch on it to calm a difficult pony – for example, if something was being done that it didn't like, such as being clipped, or having its teeth rasped. The twitch consisted of a loop of rope or leather that was twisted around the top lip, and it was believed that the pressure on the lip released substances into the blood called endorphins, which made the pony feel happier. Scientists believe chocolate has the same effect on us! Nowadays, however, most people think that twitches are cruel, so they aren't used very much.

While they are not exactly part of the five senses, ponies also seem to have a couple of extra abilities.

Time
All ponies have an acute sense of time. They know exactly when a meal is due, when it's time for them to be put out in the field, or taken back in again. And if you are late with breakfast because you overslept, they tell you about it! They will stand whinnying or, if they get really cross, may even kick at the stable door. Similarly, when they are out in wet and wild winter weather, they will be waiting at the gate for you, and if you are late they will look very hurt and upset. They won't mind you being late half so much in good weather when there is plenty of grass to eat!

Homing instinct
Many animals have a strong homing

instinct, and horses and ponies are no exception. For years, people have used this instinct when they themselves have been lost, knowing that although they do not know the way home, their horse does. Although people have carried out various experiments, no one seems to know exactly how animals do this.

Scientists think it is connected with the sense of smell, as ponies seem to be better at finding their way home when they are downwind of it, that is, when the wind is blowing from the home area toward them. It may be that their sense of smell is so good that they can actually smell their homes from miles away.

Communication and Intelligence

Communication and Intelligence

Ponies communicate their feelings to each other, and to us, by sound – whinnies, nickers, squeals and snorts – and by what is called body language, which means their bodily movements and the look in their eyes.

Pony Talk

Ponies can make a number of different noises by which they communicate. Other ponies know instinctively what the sounds mean. We have to learn them.

1. Whinny

The whinny is a long-distance communication signal that allows horses and ponies to make contact with each other, even when they cannot see each other. If you turn your pony out into the field where its friends are and they are out of sight, it will whinny anxiously and go looking for them. A mare will whinny to her foal to remind it not to stray too far away. Your pony may whinny when it sees you arrive at the yard where it lives, or, if it's kept at home, when it sees you come out of the door of the house. If you have kept it waiting for its food, it may whinny to remind you of your duties. Often a pony in a field will whinny when it hears the hooves of other ponies going along the road. So a whinny can signal pleasure, "It's good to see you," or a greeting, "Hello, who are you?," or anxiety, "Where are you?" Just as human voices are distinct, each horse or pony has a recognizable whinny that is unique to itself.

2. Nicker

The nicker is the gentle, low-pitched "woo-hoo-hoo" noise that a pony makes through its nostrils when you approach it at meal times. Ponies often greet their owners like this even if food is not offered. The sound can be very quiet, so quiet that you may just see the pony's nostrils quivering and scarcely hear any sound at all. Mares and foals greet each other in this way. Between ponies, this sound means, "I'm pleased to see you," "I don't mean you any harm," and, "I am not a threat to you." It's a cozy, friendly sound, and most pony owners think it's very good to hear it.

Curious Konik Ponies

3. Snort

The snort is a warning sound. It is made by horses and ponies blowing down their nostrils in a quick, abrupt way, a bit like a sneeze. Horses and ponies snort when they are alarmed, or suspicious of something. Often they will turn their heads toward the objects that are upsetting them, stand stock still and stare for a few seconds, with their heads held high, then snort, sometimes once, sometimes several times. After they have done this they may approach the object cautiously, stretching out their necks so they can investigate without putting themselves too near in case of danger. They may then snort again. In groups of wild horses, when the herd stallion snorts in this way, it is a signal to the other members of the herd to take notice of him.

4. Squeal

A squeal is a high-pitched sound that horses and ponies use when they confront each other. Sometimes, when two strange ponies meet they will sniff at each other, and one or both of them may squeal. This may lead to one or the other trying to bite, or possibly swinging their quarters around threatening to kick, or it may just stop at a squeal. Ponies who do know each other may also squeal, when one feels angry with the other. One pony may approach another, stretch out

its neck, lay its ears back and bare its teeth, and the other may swing its quarters around and squeal in anger.

When two stallions approach each other in a challenge for control of the herd, they squeal at each other, and this often takes the place of real fighting. Usually the stallion who squeals for the longer time is the dominant one, and the other one will walk away. This may be

because the one who squeals longer has a greater lung capacity, and is likely to be the stronger animal!

Body Language

Ponies, like people, also show their feelings by the way they behave, as well as by the sounds they make. This is called body language.

1. Ears

The position of a pony's ears tells a lot about how it is feeling. A pony in a good mood, interested in what is going on around it, will have its ears pricked forwards. Sometimes it will have one ear forwards and one ear back. This means that its attention is divided – it may be concentrating on what is happening in front of it, while half listening to something behind it or to the side. If you are riding a pony and you speak to it, it will flick an ear back to listen to you. However, when a pony lays both ears back, especially when it lays them flat back and screws up its nostrils at the same time, it means, "Look out! I'm feeling angry!" This ear position may also be accompanied by a swishing tail, which reinforces the message. So if one pony approaches another with its ears flat back, the other pony is warned, and if it doesn't want a confrontation it will walk away. However, if it is feeling angry itself, it may also lay its ears back, and there is a stand off. Usually one pony will walk away, but just occasionally there is a biting or kicking match.

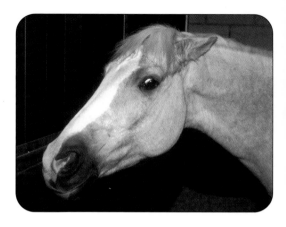

Appaloosa

2. Eyes

Appaloosa horses have a noticeable white ring around their eyes, which you can see all the time. But usually when a horse or pony shows the whites of its eyes, it is a sign of fear, and the pony is frightened of something or apprehensive about it.

3. Tail

When a pony is standing relaxed and happy its tail hangs down loosely. It is not held stiffly. When a pony walks, it lifts its tail slightly, and the tail swings gently from side to side. An Arab horse lifts its tail quite high as it moves. But its tail is still relaxed, even though it is held away from the hindquarters. But a pony that is cold and unhappy may clamp its tail down firmly against its quarters. A pony with a stiff or injured back will do the same. If a pony clamps its tail down when it is in action, it can be a sign that it is going to buck. A swishing tail (other than when it is try- ing to get rid of flies) means a pony is feeling irritable, and if it swishes its tail from side to side it can mean it is going to kick. When a pony is turned out in a field and is feeling full of the joys of spring, it will often hold its tail high up like a banner and charge around. This is called "high-tailing" and is a sign that the pony is feeling full of life and joy.

4. Swinging the Quarters Around

Some ponies, even if they don't kick, will swing their quarters around toward another pony. This is a signal that they are feeling aggressive, and a warning that they just might kick, so the other pony had better watch out!

5. Pawing the Ground

Ponies may do this in the stable, waiting at the field gate, or when you have mounted them and are standing still. It is usually a sign of impatience. When they are waiting for you in the stable or the field, if they start to paw the ground, they're saying, "Come on, get a move on, I'm waiting for you!" If you are standing still while riding them, it can also mean, "Come on, let's get on with it, I want to go home, you're wasting good eating time!" But beware – when some ponies paw the ground when you are riding them it can mean they want to get down and roll. They often like to do this when they are being ridden in the snow. So if this happens to you, get the pony moving immediately, and don't let it get any more ideas about lying down!

6. Snapping Movements of the Jaws

Young horses and ponies sometimes approach older ones with snapping movements of their jaws. This movement is different from the laying back of the ears and baring of the teeth, and it is a sign that the animal doing it is not a threat to the other, but is submissive to it. An adult horse or pony will not attack a younger one that approaches it with this snapping movement.

7. Mutual Grooming

From time to time two horses or ponies that are friends will walk up to each other and start nibbling at each other's neck, flanks or withers, as if someone had given an unseen signal. After a few minutes they will just as suddenly stop and continue grazing. It is a sign of friendship, and the ponies seem to get a lot of pleasure from it. How one knows where the other one itches is a mystery!

8. Fly Protection

In summer weather when flies are a nuisance, horses and ponies often stand in pairs, nose to tail. One pony swishes its tail to remove flies from its own flanks then helps rid the other pony of flies from its face, which is where they cause the greatest discomfort. This is a great help to both of them – a sort of mutual help society.

9. General Appearance

A pony shows its general health by its body language, too. A happy, healthy horse or pony appears relaxed and interested in everything that goes on around it. If it is with others in a field, it will be part of the group, even if some are graz-

ing a little apart from the rest. It will have clear, shining eyes and a shiny coat, even if it does get plastered with mud. Neither its eyes nor its nose will be running. It will be nicely rounded without being fat. You shouldn't be able to see its ribs, but you should be able to feel them if you prod! If you pick up a fold of skin between your thumb and forefinger and then let it go, it should spring back into place.

An unhappy or ill horse or pony will appear to be dejected. It may stand with its head hanging down, looking miserable. Often it will keep apart from other ponies. Its coat may be dull and lifeless looking, and if you pick up a fold of its skin, it may not spring back into place. This is a sign that the pony is dehydrated (lacking water). The pony may hold itself tensely, and move stiffly, if it is suffering from pain. It may lie down a lot. While it is natural for a horse or pony to rest a hind foot when it is

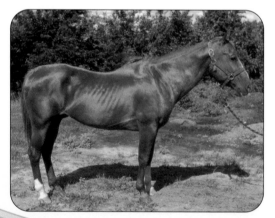

Ailing pony

Healthy pony

dozing, resting a front foot is a sign of lameness.

A Pony's Intelligence

People have different views about how intelligent horses and ponies are. Some say they are very intelligent indeed, and will work things out for themselves. Others think they are not too intelligent – if they were, why would they allow themselves to be told what to do by us? They are many times bigger, heavier and stronger than we are, so why should they do what we want? Working hard for us can't be as much fun as eating grass with their friends.

The odd thing is that horses and ponies do what we want because they are made by nature to behave in that way. It is nothing to do with intelligence. They have an instinctive wish to be told what to do. As we have seen, horses and ponies in their natural state follow the wishes of the lead horse, and anyone who doesn't soon gets put in its place. When we domesticate ponies, we take the place of that dominant animal and give the orders. Because they naturally do as they are told by the lead horse, in its absence they look to us for guidance. This is why ponies feel happy and secure when they are handled by people who are confident, and get nervous when people are timid or frightened of them. There are a few horses and ponies that don't behave in this way – these are the ones that would have been lead horses or ponies themselves. They can be very difficult for people to handle, but if you once manage to get them to do what

you want, they can be wonderful performers. Many top-class show-jumpers and racehorses fall into this category, but you need to be a very experienced rider to get the best out of them.

As with people, some horses and ponies are brighter than others. Some will learn very quickly what you want while others take a long time, and you have to be very patient with them. This not only applies to things you try to teach them when you are riding, but also

in the stable. For example, some will learn to operate things like an automatic waterer very quickly while others never learn at all. Some, unfortunately, learn how to push back the bolts of their stable doors and escape! This is why the swing type of catch, or a bolt with a hook on the end that cannot be slid when it is in the locked position, is often used in stables.

Arab horses are known for their intelligence. They seem to understand how their owners are feeling, and empathize with them. They are very sensitive to the slightest commands of their riders, and seem to know what is wanted of them almost before the rider does herself (or himself). Yet some people say they are brainless, because they will shy at a piece of paper in a hedge one day, and shy again the next day because the paper is gone. This is also true! But it may be because they seem to like things to be the same – their surroundings, their routine, their companions – and if anything changes, it upsets them.

One thing all horses and ponies are very good at doing is sizing up their humans. If you are nervous, either about handling them or riding them, they sense it. Depending on their temperament, your nervousness either makes them apprehensive too, or it makes them behave badly and bully you. This, in turn, will make you more nervous! But if you are cheerful and confident in the way you handle them and ride them, they respond to you and will happily obey your wishes.

Memory

No one disputes the fact that horses and ponies have first-class memories. If they have always been handled well and have confidence in their handler, they will trust people and behave well. If they have a bad experience they never forget it. A pony that gets upset by, for example, having to go through a gateway, has probably had something unpleasant happen to it going through a similar gateway in the past. A pony that becomes nervous when it sees a man in blue overalls has probably been treated badly by someone dressed in the same way. This ability to remember so clearly is one reason why it is so important to ensure that ponies don't have bad experiences! A farrier who handles a nervous pony roughly may make it difficult to shoe for life. One who is patient, calm and friendly gives confidence to the pony, and teaches it that shoeing is nothing to be afraid of. The same applies to getting a pony to do something it is naturally apprehensive about, such as going up the ramp of a horse trailer, or passing a noisy tractor on the road. If it has been handled well from the beginning, these things should cause no problems, but if it hasn't, it can take a very long time to re-train it.

Curiosity

Horses and ponies, like cats, have a great sense of curiosity. They need to investigate things they are suspicious of, by staring at them, sniffing at them, snorting at them, or possibly investigating them with their top lips. These actions help to calm their fears. Once they have completed their investigations and discovered that something is not harmful, they will usually ignore it. But it is partly fear that causes them to be curious about unusual objects in the first place.

This wild Brumby is very curious, but as you can see on the next page, he decides to run away.

Wild
Brumbies
running away

A Happy Home for a Pony

A Happy Home for a Pony

There are two ways of keeping a pony: in a field or in a stable. A field seems to be nearer to its natural life – it lives outside, it can feed when it likes, it can roam around and get exercise. But a pony out in a field has to cope with all kinds of weather – rain, wind, snow, burning sun – and flies. If the field is badly drained the pony may have to stand in deep mud most of the time in winter. Ponies hate mud, and it can give them mud fever, which is a soreness and inflammation of the lower part of the leg just above the hoof. So living in a field

is not quite the same as a natural life, because naturally ponies wouldn't be confined to just one field. They would move on constantly, giving them access to fresh grazing all the time, and they wouldn't have to stand around in mud.

A stable, though, is completely unnatural. The pony is shut in and cannot move around much. It can only eat when its owner feeds it, and even if it can see other ponies it is unlikely to be able to touch them and relate to them in the same way as ponies out in a field togeth-

er can do. But the pony is kept dry and warm in winter, cool in summer, and isn't tormented by flies. So which is better? Ideally, perhaps a mixture of both, so a pony is stabled most of the time in bad weather but let out into the field for some time each day so it can have some freedom. Or, if it is kept out in a field all the time, the field should have a large field shelter where it can take refuge from bad weather, hot sunshine and flies, and where it can be fed in winter.

Many people stable horses and ponies

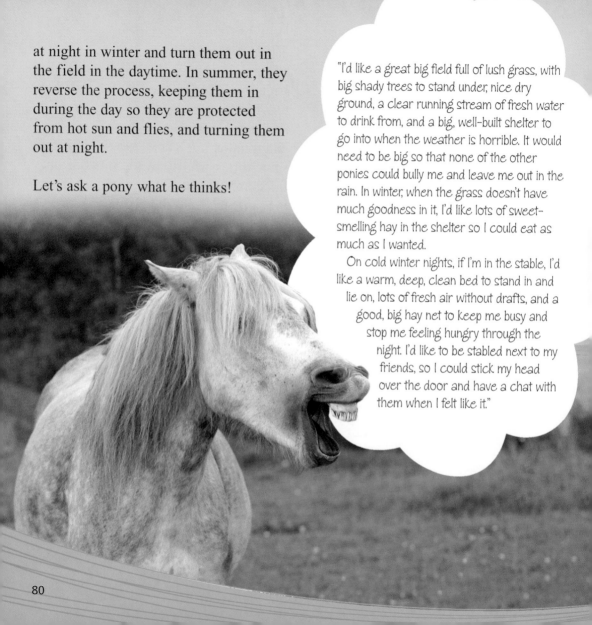

at night in winter and turn them out in the field in the daytime. In summer, they reverse the process, keeping them in during the day so they are protected from hot sun and flies, and turning them out at night.

Let's ask a pony what he thinks!

"I'd like a great big field full of lush grass, with big shady trees to stand under, nice dry ground, a clear running stream of fresh water to drink from, and a big, well-built shelter to go into when the weather is horrible. It would need to be big so that none of the other ponies could bully me and leave me out in the rain. In winter, when the grass doesn't have much goodness in it, I'd like lots of sweet-smelling hay in the shelter so I could eat as much as I wanted.

On cold winter nights, if I'm in the stable, I'd like a warm, deep, clean bed to stand in and lie on, lots of fresh air without drafts, and a good, big hay net to keep me busy and stop me feeling hungry through the night. I'd like to be stabled next to my friends, so I could stick my head over the door and have a chat with them when I felt like it."

The pony's owner may not agree about the lush grass in spring and summer, which can give the pony laminitis, but otherwise it sounds about right!

What else does a pony need to keep it happy? Like us it needs food, water, shelter, the company of its own kind, and a certain amount of freedom to do as it likes. Let's look at each of these things separately.

Food

As we have seen, ponies naturally eat grass and other plants that grow among the grass, such as dandelions and clover. Grass is not very nutritious, so in order to have enough nourishment a pony must eat a lot of it. A pony has a small stomach and a large intestine, so it eats a little at a time, but over a period it takes in a lot of bulk food. If we keep a pony in a field it can eat as much grass as it likes. In spring and summer, when the grass is growing strongly and is full of sugars, a pony can easily eat more grass

than is good for it, and can make itself ill (see previous mention!). If we keep it in a stable, then we must replace the grass with hay or haylage. A pony that doesn't do any work can live entirely on hay or haylage. But if we work it hard, then it needs extra energy, so we have to feed what is called "hard feed" – grains such as oats, barley and corn. These can be fed ready mixed in a balanced diet form as a coarse mix, or as little pellets, called nuts or cubes. A pony's digestive system, however, is not designed to cope with large amounts of this kind of food, so we have to divide it into several small feeds during the day. A pony given a large feed (or one that manages to help itself from the feed bin) can become extremely ill.

But ponies do like fresh, succulent foods, so a diet of hay and hard feed can become a bit boring. A few treats like carrots sliced lengthways (ponies can choke on chunks of carrot), sliced apple, or, best of all, some time spent grazing each day, are very much appreciated.

Water

In the wild, ponies tend to go two or three times a day to a source of water, and have a good long drink. There is quite a lot of water in the grass they eat, too. If we keep them in a stable and feed them hay they need to drink more than they would if they were out in a field. If a pony takes a long drink when its stomach is full of hard feed, the water can wash the food down too quickly, and a blockage may occur in the intestines. The pony then suffers from colic (stomachache), which can be very serious. So it is best to provide a constant supply of water, so the pony can drink small amounts whenever it wants.

Shelter

A few very small, tough ponies that grow long, waterproof coats, such as Shetlands, can withstand all kinds of weather, but most ponies need some kind of shelter from wind, rain, snow and hot summer sun. They don't mind the cold, as long as the weather is dry and not windy. Trees and thick hedges provide some shelter, but if they lose their leaves in winter they are not much use. This is why field shelters are a good idea if ponies have to live outside all the time.

Clipped ponies, or those with thin skins and coats, can be given some protection from the weather with New Zealand rugs. These are lined and waterproof, and are held in place by leg straps as well as surcingles, so that when the pony rolls they stay in place.

Company

We have seen that ponies are herd animals that live together in family groups. Not only does the group provide company, it also gives protection. In their natural state ponies are preyed upon by wolves and other animals. When they are in a group, some animals can relax for part of the time while the others keep guard. On its own, it has no one to keep a look-out for danger, so a pony must be constantly vigilant. Nowadays, if we keep a pony out in a field, we know it isn't going to be pounced on by a pack of wolves, but the pony doesn't know that, and the old, hereditary instincts remain. So a pony on its own may well be nervous, anxious and unhappy. Unlike us, it can't reason that there is no need for it to feel this way. Its feelings are instinctive, and it cannot control them. But as soon as it has the company of other ponies, it automatically feels safer, and therefore happier and more relaxed.

Ideally ponies should be kept in groups, but this is not always possible. Even one companion makes a big difference to a pony's happiness and well-being, and this companion doesn't have to be another riding pony; a retired pony or horse is just as suitable. If the company of another horse or pony is not possible, then that of other animals, such as cattle, sheep, donkeys or goats, is better than nothing. Cattle and sheep can keep a lonely pony company out in the field , but a pet goat or donkey can be stabled next to the pony and they can become good friends. (Of course, there's another problem here; goats and donkeys are herd animals, too, and it is kinder to them to keep more than one!) Family pets such as dogs and cats also get along with horses, and can provide some company in the stable. If there are no other animals, then the pony needs lots of visits from people during the day.

Nowadays, many people consider it is cruel to keep a pony on its own. In some countries, such as Sweden, the government is considering passing laws to ban

people from keeping ponies on their own.

Freedom

Ponies naturally roam over quite long distances, so to keep one cooped up in a stable, or even a field, is unnatural. In its natural life a pony has the freedom to do as it pleases, and it always has clean grazing to crop. But a field soon gets covered with droppings. And ponies graze very unevenly (which is one reason why farmers don't like them grazing their fields), eating some areas right down and leaving clumps of coarse, unpalatable grasses and weeds in others. They leave their droppings in these areas, too. Ponies excrete worm eggs in their droppings, and can re-infest themselves by grazing affected areas. So, especially in a small field, the droppings should be cleaned up regularly.

To keep the grazing as clean as possible, pony fields should ideally be rested every few weeks, and then grazed by cattle and sheep before being used by

ponies again. This way the grazing is evened out, and doesn't become sour or infested by worms. Topping (mowing the tops off the grass and other plants) also helps to even out the grazing, and prevents weeds such as thistles from seeding. Harrowing breaks up the clumps of droppings, exposing them to the sun, which will kill the worm eggs. A pony's field needs a lot of attention if the pony is to live a healthy and natural life!

But any kind of turnout area is better than nothing. A pony should be turned out for some time each day, even if it's only an hour or two, to stretch its legs and behave exactly as it likes. One of a pony's favorite activities is to get down and roll, usually in the muddiest part of the field, making lots of work for you cleaning it up! Out in the field it can roll as much as it likes. If it is out with other ponies, they can nuzzle and groom each other, and they may play or go for a gallop and a buck or two. It's like you being let out of school and running around the playground, talking to your friends, or

playing games with them. You'd get very bored and fed up if you didn't have some freedom to do as you like, and ponies are just the same.

Avoiding Boredom

When a pony has to be kept in a stable, perhaps to keep it from eating too much spring or summer grass, it easily gets bored. Frequent visits from its owner help. Ponies enjoy human company, and if you chat to one and give it a friendly pat on the neck it will appreciate it, even if you don't bring a tidbit. Though, of course, they love having tidbits as often as possible! If a pony can see other ponies from its stable, and watch people coming and going, that will also keep it interested. If the pony doesn't need its food rationed, picking at a hay bag keeps it occupied. If it is on a diet and can't have too much hay you can give it small amounts of barley straw to eat. This provides very little nourishment, but if you scatter it on the ground ponies enjoy rooting about in it and eating some of it. As long as they don't eat too much it shouldn't do any harm. But don't give a pony wheat straw to eat, as this can give it colic. You can also buy "horse toys" to amuse horses and ponies kept in stables. These include soccer balls, which some ponies enjoy playing with, and flavored mineral licks that either fix to the wall or dangle from the ceiling, which ponies enjoy licking and chewing.

Keeping Flies at Bay

Some ponies suffer terribly from persecution by flies in summer. Ideally they should have shelter to escape from them, but if this is not possible there are a number of other things you can do to help.

1. Fly Repellents

These are chemicals that you wipe onto the pony's coat with a cloth or a sponge. Some are natural substances like oil of citronella, while others are powerful chemicals that need to be handled with care. You wipe them on the parts of a pony that its tail cannot reach, like its head and underbelly. You must be very careful when you put them on the pony's head that you do not get any of the substance in its eyes or on its muzzle. Some fly repellents are sprayed on, but not all ponies will tolerate this. But if this is the case, you can spray them onto the cloth, and then wipe them on in the same way as the others.

2. Fly Fringes

Various kinds of fly fringes are available. Some attach to a pony's head collar and some can be worn on their own, but they all have strings of soft material that hang down over the pony's eyes and move when it does or when the wind blows, thereby swishing any flies away.

Fly fringe

Fly Mask

3. Fly Masks

These are hoods made of fine mesh, which may just cover the pony's eyes, or may cover the whole face, including the ears and nose. They look a bit frightening, but ponies soon get used to them and enjoy wearing them in hot, fly-ridden weather. The hoods keep all the flies away from the pony's eyes and face, which is where they torment ponies the most. They can also be worn when the pony is ridden. (See Headshaking, page 142.)

Ponies and
People

Ponies and People

Look at a friend who's about your height and weight standing by a pony. How many times larger than your friend is the pony? How much heavier do you suppose it is?

The average pony of, say, 13.2 hands high, weighs about 660 pounds (300 kg). Isn't it amazing that you, or your friend, can tell the pony what to do, and it obeys you, even when it goes against its natural instincts or wishes to do so? When you think about it, it's all a bit of a miracle, isn't it? Because, if this were not the case, the whole of human history would have been different. No one would have been able to use horses and ponies over the centuries for work, and you would not be able to ride one today. Because we take the place of the leader of the herd, a pony expects us to tell it what to do, and it is quite happy to follow our wishes. (See A Pony's Intelligence, page 71.) For this reason,

when we handle ponies, out attitude toward them is very important. No matter how we are feeling, we should always try to be calm, quiet, gentle and firm without being aggressive. If our attitude is always the same, the pony feels safe with us, and we give it a sense of security. Then it is happy to accept us as its boss and leader.

Your tone of voice is important when you speak to a pony. It should be quiet, firm and confident. You should never get angry or shout and scream at a pony, even if it is naughty and needs telling off. Shouting upsets a pony and frightens it, and if you act differently from the way you usually do it will think there is something wrong.

Discipline

So how should you discipline a pony? No matter how much you love it, there will be times when it is naughty and needs telling off. A firm "No!" will often do the trick, sometimes reinforced

with a slap on the neck if this is necessary. And you have to make your pony obey your wishes, otherwise you cannot have a partnership. You must be the boss, not the pony. But you cannot assert your authority over a pony by bullying, shouting at or hitting it. You need to be firm, and also consistent. There's no point in scolding a pony for doing something one day and then letting it get away with it the next. You also need to be fair. If your pony pulls you toward its feed bucket, and you know it's likely to be very hungry because you've been

working it hard, it's not fair to scold it. If, however, it pulls you toward hedges, clumps of grass or bracken fern when you're riding, hoping to snatch a mouthful, then you should keep it from doing so as soon as possible. It shouldn't be allowed to eat at all while you are riding. A pony that thinks it can put its head down to graze when it feels like it becomes very difficult to ride! And it should never be allowed to snatch at bracken fern, whether it is being ridden or not, as bracken fern is poisonous.

If You Are Nervous

If, for any reason, you feel afraid of a pony, and you cannot overcome this enough to hide the feeling when you handle it or ride it, then you shouldn't be handling it or riding it. If it is a difficult or aggressive pony (and there aren't many of these around), and it senses your nervousness, it will try to bully you. It needs a more experienced handler who is not afraid of it, and who will tell it firmly what to do. And you need

to handle a quiet, gentle, good-natured pony to build up your confidence. If you are nervous about riding a pony because it is too lively, then you need to change to a quiet, reliable pony that makes you feel safe.

Routine

Ponies, like most animals, love routine. They like everything to be done at the same time each day – mealtimes, riding times, being put out in the field and being brought in again. So although there may be days when this is not possible, try your very best to map out a timetable and stick to it. Think about it before you commit yourself, because the timetable has to suit you as well as the pony. But once you have worked it out, do your best to be consistent. Ponies don't understand Sunday morning sleeping in, or vacations, or at any other special days – to them, each day is the same, therefore they expect breakfast (and every other meal) at the same time. Some people are like this, too!

Making Friends With a Strange Pony

When you approach a strange pony in a field, walk confidently up to it, approaching its head from the side. That way it can see you easily and will not be startled by your appearance. Hold out your hand as if offering a tidbit, and the pony is likely to raise its head and prick its ears forward in anticipation. When you do stretch your hand out toward the pony, curl up your fingers and let it sniff the back of your hand. This will protect you in case it tries to take a nip. Most ponies don't nip, but if you don't know the pony, don't take the chance. If your fingers are held out, at the worst you could lose one or more; if you offer the back of your hand, the worst that can happen is a graze of the skin. Ponies aren't monsters that bite, but some do try to nip, and they have very powerful teeth and jaws, so if you're unsure of one, it's better to be careful.

As you approach the pony, speak confidently to it. Let it sniff your hand, and once it has done so, if it looks good-natured, give it a pat on the neck while you are still speaking to it. Then, if you want to give it a tidbit, offer the treat on the palm of your hand. If there are other ponies in the field, offering tidbits can cause problems, though, as they will all want one, and they may come charging up and then all mill around trying to nip each other, and possibly you too. So if there are several ponies in a field it is better not to offer a tidbit – save it until you have the pony on its own. Some ponies like to have their heads and necks stroked, some don't, and some seem indifferent to it. When you are getting to know a pony you have to find out what it likes. Some like being rubbed on their foreheads and around their ears, while others prefer

to have their withers scratched. If you're prepared to spend time doing this, while speaking to the pony in a friendly tone, you are well on the way to becoming fast friends.

Handling a Pony in a Stable
Most ponies you will come across will be accustomed to being handled and will be well-mannered. So as you approach the stable door, over which the pony is likely to be watching, wondering what goodies you may be bringing it, speak to the pony. When you open the door, if it doesn't move back, push it gently on its chest and say, "Back." Go into the stable and close the door behind you. Give the pony a friendly pat, and then put

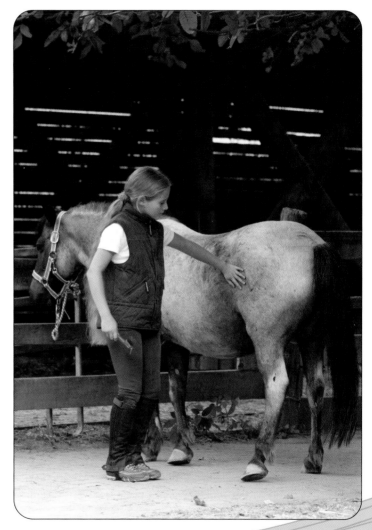

on its head collar and tie it up if you need to, and do whatever you came into the stable to do.

If the pony is standing in your way, say, "Move over," and push its hindquarters in the direction in which you want it to move. Most ponies understand this and readily obey, but a few may decide to take no notice of you. If this is the case, repeat the command and push a bit more firmly. When the pony responds and moves over, give it a pat on the neck and say, "Good boy," in a warm, encouraging tone of voice, different from the one you used for the command.

1. When Feeding

If you come into the stable to feed a pony you will not need to tie it up, though you may need to push it out of the way until you've had time to tip the feed into the feeder, or put the feeding bowl on the ground! Some ponies are well-mannered and will wait, but some get quite pushy. When one behaves like this, don't let it bully you. Say, "No!," or, "Wait!" and push it out of the way until you have put the feed down. When it obeys, pat it and praise it. They soon learn!

2. When Grooming

It is best to tie up a pony while you are grooming it. Even the best-mannered animals are likely to try to wander around otherwise. Tie the pony to a tying ring with a quick-release knot. Many people tie a loop of string to the tying ring and then attach the pony's rope to that. This is because there is always the possibility of a pony panicking and pulling backwards to try and get free. If it's tied to a piece of string, the string will break, and the pony will not injure itself or damage the stable. If the pony is restless, give it a small haynet to keep it occupied while you groom it and pick out its feet.

While grooming, handle the pony confidently, and use firm strokes with the brush. If the strokes are too light, you will tickle the pony. If it starts to make a

Quick-release knot

face, this may be the reason! A thin-skinned pony in its summer coat can be quite sensitive around its head, under its tummy and on the insides of its back legs. If this is the case, try to avoid using the dandy brush in these areas, and use a body brush. If you need to remove mud, use a rubber curry comb, which is less scratchy than a dandy brush.

If the pony has a long mane and tail that have gotten very tangled, brush out as much of the tangles as you can and then undo knots with your fingers. Don't tug a mane comb through the hair. This will be as uncomfortable for your pony as someone pulling your own hair is, and if you do it repeatedly the pony will become sore and the mane and tail will look ragged and untidy.

When you walk around the back of a strange pony, run your hand down the top of its tail. If it is at all inclined to kick, this will make it change its mind, as it is much more likely to tuck its bottom in, away from the pressure of your hand, than to kick out.

To pick up a foot, first run your hand down the back of its leg, then move your hand around to the front of the leg just above the hoof, so you can hold the hoof when it lifts it up. (If it doesn't lift it up

when you do this, say, "Up," and give a little tug at it.) If the pony is putting its weight on the foot you want to pick up, lean into it slightly with your shoulder to push its weight onto the leg on the opposite side and try again.

3. When Mucking Out

It is a good idea to tie up the pony while you muck it's stall out. It makes life much easier for you if you can go in and out with the barrow without having to shut the stable door each time. Giving the pony a small haynet will keep it occupied.

Handling Ponies in a Field

If the pony is in a field with a lot of others, handling it can be difficult if the others all come galloping up to join in the act. Sometimes just waiting for a while does the trick. They soon realize that there isn't any food being offered, and may just get bored and walk away. If they do all charge up to you, wave your arms at them and shout, "Go away!" If

necessary you can slap a pony that comes too close on its nose. But if you know they are likely to be difficult, it is best to get a friend to help you. That way, one of you can catch the pony you want while the other shoos the other ponies away.

Unless all the ponies in the field are very quiet, it's easier to lead your pony through the gate and tie it up (using a loop of string) outside the field if you need to do anything to it. If, however, the gate leads onto a busy road, it is much safer to lead the pony back to the

stable yard and attend to it there.

To turn a pony out into a field in which there are other ponies, lead it through the gate, keeping hold of both the gate and the pony. Once inside the field, turn the pony around to face the gate while you fasten it in case any of the ponies gets out. Then lead your pony further into the field, turn it around again to face back to the gate, slip off the head collar and then stand out of the way in case it whips around quickly and charges off to join its friends. If you know the other ponies are likely to cause problems, take a friend with you to help.

Catching a Pony

Some ponies will canter happily up to the gate when you call them and then stand still while you slip on their head collars. Some ponies will stand still and look up as you approach them, and wait for you to slip on their head collars. And some ponies won't! Some will take one look at you and hurtle off across the field, and maybe gallop around and around while you trail after them. It can be very frustrating and exhausting!

It is usually a waste of time and energy to follow a pony that runs away from you. That sort of pony seems to think it is all a good game, and will wait until you're almost upon them before galloping off again. And there is no way you can keep up with them! Don't get drawn into this – it's much too much fun for the pony, and none at all for you. So what can you do?

Sometimes it helps to offer a tidbit, such as a slice of apple or a carrot. If you approach the pony with the head collar hidden behind your back, holding out your other hand with the tidbit on it, the pony may let you slip on the head collar. Then you can give it the tidbit, and pat it and tell it what a good pony it is, in a warm and encouraging tone of voice (even if you feel annoyed with it!) Don't give the tidbit until the head collar is safely fastened on, or it may charge off again before you have a chance to do so.

Some ponies will come if you carry a

bucket with feed in it, especially something like pony nuts which you can rattle as you call the pony's name. Again, put the head collar on the pony before offering it the feed. And do give it the feed, because if you cheat and take the bucket away again, next time it's not going to come when it sees the bucket! It's all a question of reward for good behavior, or, if you prefer, bribery!

With a pony you know to be difficult, visit it several times without even trying to catch it, just offering a tidbit and speaking encouragingly. Try to stroke and pat the pony as you talk to it. If you can do this several times without it running off, next time you visit try hiding the head collar behind your back, and as you speak to the pony stroke its neck and slip on the head collar before offering the tidbit.

Although it is usually safer to turn out a pony without a head collar on, if one is really difficult to catch, then leave on the head collar and have a short length of rope hanging from it to give you

something to grab if you manage to get close enough. You can then clip on a proper head collar rope that you've had hidden in your pocket as soon as you have caught the pony. It's difficult to lead a pony by a short rope, because it can easily pull away from you, and you probably won't be able to keep hold of it.

Another way of catching a difficult pony is to provoke its curiosity. Go into the field with a bucket of feed, and something to eat yourself, such as candies with rustling papers. Sit down in the field and rattle the feed in the bucket, rustle your papers, and maybe eat a candy or two. After a while, the chances are that the pony will wonder what on earth is going on and will come to investigate (ponies have a great sense of curiosity), and when it does you can

grab hold of it and then give it the feed. Sometimes a difficult pony will follow another pony who is easy to catch. Even if it doesn't allow you to catch hold of it, it may follow loose and go into its stable. Of course, you can only try this method if the stable is near the paddock, and if there is no possibility of the pony getting out onto a road. It's not ideal, because as you don't actually catch the pony you are, in a way, giving in to it, but if you are really desperate it may be one way to get it out of the field.

If you know a pony is really difficult, you could try turning it out in a small paddock on its own. It will then be much more likely to want to come in and join its friends. If even this doesn't work, get someone to help you by leading another pony up to yours to entice it, and with luck you'll be able to grab it before it realizes it's been tricked.

Leading a Pony

Leading a pony, like everything else connected with handling one, is usually done from its left side. This dates back to the days of knights on horseback, who carried swords on their left sides so they could draw them with their right hands.

If you have a sword hanging down your left side, you have to mount by putting your left foot in the stirrup, which means standing on the left-hand side of the pony. Although all this was important several hundred years ago, and isn't now, we still follow the tradition. To lead a pony, then, stand on its left-hand side, hold the lead rope in your right hand high up near its head collar, and hold the end of the rope in your left hand. Say, "Walk on," and walk briskly forwards. Don't look back at the pony, and it will follow you. (If you do look back, it's likely to stop.) It is very unlikely that the pony will misbehave, but if it does, then let go with your right hand, keeping hold of the end of the rope with your left, and it will run around you in a circle rather than charging off. Once it's settled down, take hold again with your right hand up by the head collar and start again.

Does a Pony Feel Affection for its Owner?

Some people say ponies are incapable of feeling affection, but others disagree. Certainly some ponies seem to enjoy their owners' company, and will nuzzle them even when food is not offered. Most ponies are pleased to see their owners, and will say so by a gentle nicker through their nostrils as you approach. How friendly a pony is depends partly on the relationship its owner creates with it. If you just ride your pony and care for it, without taking time to speak to it or to visit it just for the pleasure of being with it, then you don't have much time to build up a friendship. But if you do take the time to make friends, talking to your pony and stroking it when you visit, your pony will respond, and your partnership will become much more rewarding.

However, if a pony goes to a new home, it won't pine for its owner in the way that a dog or cat would. It will be a little unsettled at first, with the new surroundings and new companions, but provided it is well cared for it will soon become happy with its new life.

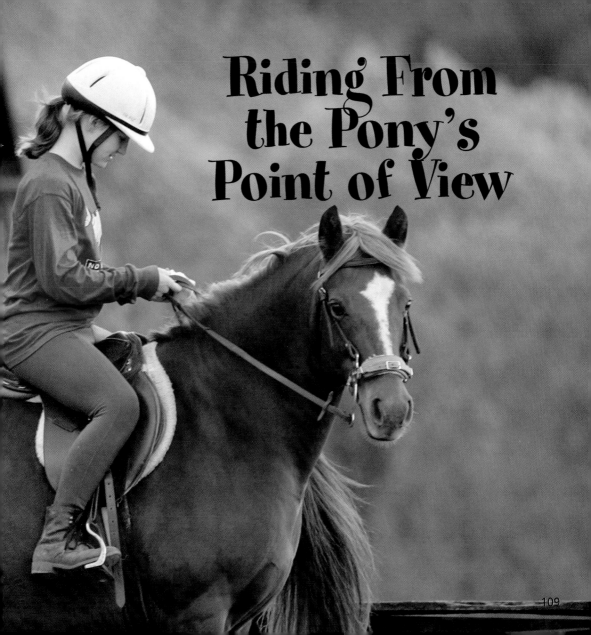

Riding From the Pony's Point of View

Riding From the Pony's Point of View

Remember the pony's natural life? It's quite a lazy one. Walking slowly around, cropping grass, occasionally resting, sometimes having a bit of fun with its friends.

Imagine you're that pony. Now think what it must be like to carry a weight on your back, sometimes for long periods of time, to gallop and jump, to go where and at what paces your rider tells you. You may be feeling full of energy and want to canter and buck when you're told to walk or trot sedately down the road. Or you may feel tired, and your back and leg muscles might be aching because you've been working harder than usual, and you may not want to go around yet another set of jumps. Yet you have to do it, because that's what you're being told to do. It's all very different from your natural life, and it can be very hard work. But this is the kind of life we expect our ponies to lead, and if they occasionally act up, we wonder what's wrong with them, and may punish them for their bad behavior. No wonder they are sometimes bewildered by the way we treat them.

So, when you are riding a pony, try to think how what you are asking it to do must seem to it. If you spend a lot of time schooling it, trotting endless circles, or going over and over the same set of jumps, it's bound to get bored and fed up. If you always go the same route when you are out trail riding, and always trot up the same hill, or canter on the same stretch of grass, it will assume that that is the thing to do, and if one day you decide to walk up that hill, or on that stretch of grass, it will dance around, wanting to set off. It's never a good idea to always do the same things in the same places. The pony will start to anticipate your wishes, and then won't listen to you if you decide to do something different. Or, if one day someone else rides it, it will assume they want to do the same thing, too, and may take them by surprise. So try to vary your trail rides and your schooling sessions, so you are always giving the commands, and not letting the pony assume what

your wishes are. And if it has been working hard, let it have a rest from time to time. Walk on a loose rein and let it stretch its neck out to relax the muscles. Let it canter for fun.

Always ride with some consideration for your pony's level of fitness. If it has been spending a lazy time out in the field for weeks, you can't just plunk a

saddle on it and expect it to go on a 20-mile trail ride. It would be like you trying to go on a long-distance walk carrying a pack if you hadn't gotten any exercise for weeks. If you were fit and had built up to the exercise gradually, you would probably manage, but if you weren't very fit you'd get blisters, your muscles would ache, you might strain a muscle, tendon or ligament, and you'd get extremely tired. An unfit pony feels practically the same. It needs to start with about half an hour of walking exercise a day for a week or so before you gradually increase the length of time and start introducing short trots. And you shouldn't be doing fast work until your pony has been working through its fitness program for six weeks or so.

So if you want to go for long trail rides, or compete in shows or gymkhanas, think of your pony as an athlete, and carry out a fitness program before asking it to work really hard and give of it best.

Fitness Program for a Pony that's Been Resting Outdoors

Weeks 1 - 3
Daily walking exercise, starting with half an hour a day and increasing to one and a half hours.

Weeks 4 - 6
Continue with the walking, but add short periods of steady trotting up hills, gradually increasing the length of time you trot and the number of periods you do it. Toward the end of this time, include some short, slow canters.

Week 7 Onwards
Introduce some longer canters uphill. As the pony gets fitter, do a couple of long, fast canters each week, walking and trotting and doing short canters on other days.

While you are carrying out this fitness program, the pony's hard feed will need to be increased, too, to cope with the extra work you are asking it to do. At the end of 12 weeks you will have a really fit pony that can compete in many activities. You may not want an animal that is so fit, as they can be quite a handful to ride, so if you only want a pony that's capable of doing medium-length trail rides, you could just carry out the program up to the six weeks stage. Once a pony is fit, riding it two or three times a week will keep it reasonably fit, but not capable of really hard work.

Riding With Consideration
A considerate rider can make an enormous difference to a pony's comfort and well-being. Contrast these two people. The first hops around trying to mount, heaves herself into the saddle, pulling it over in the process, and sits down with a thump. Then she claps the pony in the ribs with her heels, yanks on its mouth to turn its head around, and sets off for a

ride. Right from the start she goes at a fast pace, giving the pony's muscles no time to warm up (the athlete again). When trotting she flops and bangs onto the saddle, and when cantering she bounces up and down, inflicting more thumps on the pony's back with each stride. To stop she pulls hard on its mouth. When jumping, she doesn't lean forward until she has cleared the jump, but balances herself by pulling on the reins, unbalancing the pony and hurting its mouth. She may make an unfit pony work hard and fast so it gets out of breath and sweats a lot, and keeps going fast right up until the time they get home. Then she gets off her dripping pony, hauls its tack off and either leaves it in the stable or turns it out into the field, still wet with sweat. The pony has a sore mouth, a sore back, aching muscles, and may get a chill if the weather is cold.

The second person is a considerate rider. If she knows she cannot spring

An example of bad riding

lightly up to mount she uses a mounting block so she doesn't pull the saddle over. She lowers herself lightly into the saddle, gathers her reins, squeezes gently with her legs, speaks a kind word or two to the pony, and sets off at a walk. She walks for a mile or so to warm up the pony's muscles before doing any faster work. Her aids (the signals a rider gives to tell a pony what to do) are as light as possible, and she keeps a light hand on the reins unless it is necessary to do otherwise. She rises just a little out of the saddle at the trot, and sits down again gently. She sits well down to canter, and when galloping raises herself out of the saddle (called forward position) to take the weight off the pony's back. She rides the pony

within the limits of its fitness, that is, she doesn't ask it to do anything it isn't ready for. When jumping she leans forward until the pony has landed and started to move forward again, so as not to pull on its mouth. If she is going fast and the pony gets a bit strong, she does not yank at its mouth, but closes her legs onto its sides and give a series of steady pulls, possibly reinforced with a "whoa." When the pony obeys her aids, she relaxes them. After a schooling session she lets the pony stretch its neck and walk on loose reins for a while to relax its muscles and cool down. And at the end of any ride, she walks for the last mile or so to cool the pony and not bring it in sweating. When they get back home and she removes the tack, she brushes the pony down, checks its feet for any stones it may have picked up, and makes sure it is comfortable before turning it out or leaving it in the stable.

If you were a pony, which rider would you prefer?

The Pony's Tack

Let's start right at the beginning, with the pony's tack. Tack should fit properly, and be well cared for. Grease and mud should be removed from the leather so they don't rub the pony's skin, and then the leather should be saddle soaped well to keep it supple and soft. This not only makes it more comfortable for the pony, but it also keeps you safe, for neglected tack can break and could cause an accident. The bit should be wide enough not to pinch the corners of the pony's mouth and adjusted to the correct height in its mouth. A snaffle bit should just wrinkle the corners of a pony's mouth; a Pelham bit sits a little lower. The throatlash should be loose enough for you to put a hand between it and the pony's head; the noseband should allow two fingers. The browband shouldn't pinch the pony's ears, nor be so tight that it pulls the bridle forwards.

The saddle should fit your pony. Ponies, and saddles, come in different widths, and you need one that is the correct width for the pony. When the saddle is sitting on the pony's back the padding should be in contact with the pony, but there should be a gap all the way along the gullet of the saddle from the front (pommel) to the back (cantle) so it doesn't press on the pony's spine. If you use a numnah, this too should be pulled up into the gullet of the saddle so it doesn't press tightly on the pony's withers. Every so often the stuffing in the saddle's panels may need renewing – this is a job for a saddler. The girth should fit comfortably, and should be kept clean so it doesn't rub the pony. The saddle must be girthed up in the right place (the little hollow in the area between the pony's chest and forelegs and the roundness of its tummy) so it doesn't rub on the muscle above the elbow. If a girth is inclined to rub, then an Atherstone girth, which is shaped so it is narrower near the pony's elbows, or a sheepskin sleeve over the girth, may be the answer.

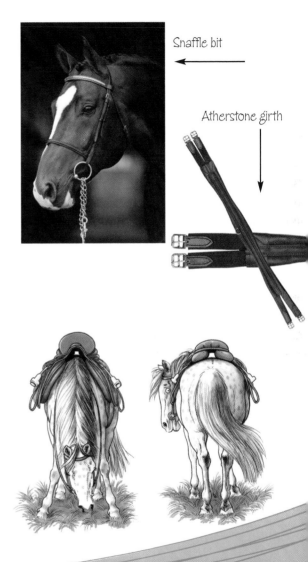

Snaffle bit

Atherstone girth

Think About Your Pony as You Ride

You want your pony to enjoy your trail ride, schooling session, or whatever else you may be participating in as much as you do, so spare a thought for its feelings as you ride.

Trail Riding

If you always go the same old route, you're both likely to get bored. Sometimes you have to go along the same bit of road to get to a bridle path or public land along which you want to ride, but try to vary the overall route. Vary, also, the places where you trot and canter. This, too, can be difficult, because there may be only a few places where you can do these things, but try to change it as much as possible. Walk on a favorite trotting or cantering place, trot where you usually canter, or don't start your trot or canter until you're halfway up the hill you normally trot or canter all the way up.

To add interest to a trail ride, you can practice a little schooling on a quiet bridleway where there is no traffic. Try doing a half-pass across the track, or practice reining back or turns on the haunches and forehand. You may even find a small area, such as a clearing in the woods, where you can trot a few circles. All this will keep the pony alert, and listening to you for your aids.

Ponies love a good canter or a gallop, and riders enjoy it, too! So, if you have a safe place, ideally on a smooth piece of soft ground free from tree roots and rabbit holes, and preferably going slightly uphill, you can let your pony have its head and go for a good gallop or fast canter. (If you go uphill, it's easier to stop a pony that's enjoying itself a little too much!) But don't do this every time you go out, or even every time you ride over that particular stretch of country. Take note, too, of the ground conditions. In winter, deep mud may make it unsuitable for cantering. In summer, it may be baked hard, like concrete, and this is not good for the pony's legs.

Where is it safe to trot and canter? If

you have to ride on a busy road (and it's much better to avoid that if possible), it's best to keep to a walk, and keep well to the side of the road. If there is traffic around, you then have a little more space to react if anything upsets the pony – such as a bag or paper fluttering in the hedge, or a startled bird flying up – and makes it shy. While you should be a confident rider, it is not sensible to take any risks when out riding on the roads. The safety of both you and your pony must come first.

You can trot safely on a quiet road or bridle path, along a level or an uphill stretch. Trotting steadily uphill is a good way of getting a pony fit. But don't trot an unfit pony for long distances along a hard road, as this can cause strains on its legs. You can also trot along grass tracks, or other tracks, but avoid those with lots of loose stones, potholes or tree roots, and head to where it is much safer to walk. Trotting downhill can help

to balance a pony, but it's really an activity for an experienced rider. An inexperienced rider on an unschooled pony can become very unbalanced trotting downhill.

And cantering? Save this for soft ground, such as along the edge of a field, or on a track with a smooth, soft surface. Cantering or galloping a pony on hard ground can injure its legs. You should never canter or gallop on a grass shoulder of the road, nor on a hard-surfaced road. Both are dangerous if traffic comes along. A cantering pony can get over-excited and become uncontrollable. Cantering on the hard-surfaced road is dangerous for other reasons, too. It jars the pony's legs and the pony may slip on the hard surface and fall.

While you should only canter on soft ground, don't trot or canter through deep mud. It can become very slippery, and it may well conceal hidden holes in the ground, which can bring your pony down and injure both of you.

Trail Riding in Bad Weather

Heavy Rain

Sometimes we have to ride in the rain, but most ponies don't enjoy being out in heavy, pouring rain. Most humans don't, either! It's up to you whether or not you go out in a downpour, but if you do, remember the following points:

1. Soft ground will become softer, and may be very muddy and slippery.

2. Traffic on the roads will make swishing sounds that may spook your pony.

3. Vehicles will have lights on which can also spook your pony.

4. When you get home, you will have to get your pony as clean and dry as possible, before you leave it.

5. Your tack will need a lot of hard work to make the soaking wet leather soft and supple again.

Strong Winds

Riding in strong winds can be dangerous. Some ponies get very silly in windy weather, and can be difficult to control. In addition, plastic bags and other litter may blow into your path, or things may clatter around, which may upset your pony. If you're riding near trees, remember that pieces of branch can come crashing down and injure you or your pony. So if you do ride in windy weather take extra care, and if the wind is very strong, it is best to stay home.

Snow and Ice

If snow is wet, it compacts into balls in the pony's hooves, raising its feet off the ground. Trying to walk in this state, a pony can easily slip, or strain its fetlocks.

Rubbing the inside of the hoof with grease such as lard can help prevent this from happening. Very cold, dry snow does not form into balls as easily.

One thing to watch out for in snow is that ponies love to roll in it. So if your pony halts, and starts pawing at the ground, send it on urgently, as otherwise it may go down and roll. If it does get down, you will have to hop off, but even if you get out of the way quickly the pony can break the saddle's tree (the inner framework on which the saddle is built), and a new saddle is very expensive.

Ice is very dangerous, as ponies slide and cannot keep their footing. Studs in the shoes may help, but ponies often fall when ridden over ice, and if they go down on their knees they can damage them severely. So it is best never to ride on ice.

Fog

Riding in fog is only safe if you can stay off the road and know the ground on which you are riding well. In thick fog, even this isn't safe. Never, ever, ride on a road in poor visibility, whether in fog or the gloomy darkness of winter mornings and evenings. Even if both you and your pony wear reflective clothing, it is still too dangerous.

Hot and Humid Weather

Think about your pony's welfare on hot summer days, especially when the weather is humid. If possible, ride early in the morning or in the evening, when it is cooler. Some rides, such as trails through woods, will offer more shade

than others, so choose those if you can. Go for a shorter ride than usual, and do more walking, so your pony doesn't get too hot and sweaty. When you return from your ride, sponge down its sweaty parts – the underside of the neck, the saddle patch, around the girth area and between its back legs – with lukewarm water. If you prepare a bucketful before you go out and stand it in the sun, it will warm up by the time you have returned, especially if it is in a black bucket. This will refresh your pony without chilling

it. Remove the surplus water with a sweat scraper, or with the side of your hand. Don't let the pony drink too much at one time, either, if you have come back from a long, hard day. A pony should not be offered water if it is breathing heavily after hard work. Wait until its breathing has returned to normal, and then offer just half a bucketful, preferably of lukewarm water. Wait 20 to 30 minutes before offering another half bucketful, and then another 20 to 30 minutes before letting it drink as much as it likes.

Schooling Sessions

You may do schooling just to make your pony more supple and obedient, or you may be getting it ready for a competition such as showing, a gymkhana, show jumping, dressage, and so on. Try to keep your schooling sessions short – no more than 30 minutes at a time. Every so often, when working your pony intensively in the ring, let it relax for a few minutes and walk around on a loose rein so it can stretch its neck out and ease its muscles. When practicing jumping, start over low poles and gradually build up to higher and more difficult jumps. Don't ask too much of the pony too soon. And don't start schooling over jumps until the pony is going well and is obedient on the ground.

The most difficult type of jump for a

pony is a high single pole with no ground line. So always lay another pole on the ground to form a ground line, and try to fill in the area under the pole with something, even if it's only brush such as hedge clippings. Straw bales make good jumps. The action of jumping always involves a certain amount of width, as well as height, so a spread fence is easier for a pony to jump than an upright. When you are constructing a course of jumps, remember to work out the number of strides before each fence as you approach it, because if you get this wrong, the pony will not be able to jump at its best.

Remember, also, when schooling, that if the pony is not used to the work, its muscles will ache just like yours do when you're performing a task for the first time, or one that you haven't done for a while, so give it a bit of a rest from time to time, letting it walk on a loose rein or have a gentle canter just to relax its muscles.

Try to vary the work as much as possible. If you're trotting circles, turn across the center, stop and do a rein back. Walk across the diagonal, do a turn on the forehand, then trot a straight line before doing more circles. Try alternating collection and extension, and changing the pace frequently at the markers around the ring. If you don't have a proper school, use landmarks such as a bush, tree or fence post as places to change the pace or direction. And don't do schooling every day or every time you ride. No matter how hard you may be practicing for an event, take some days off and go out for a trail ride. And give your pony a complete day off once a week or so, when it can just enjoy itself in the field with its friends.

Riding in a Group

Ponies like to be with their friends, and your pony will enjoy going out for a ride with other ponies. But, in a group there may also be ponies it doesn't like very much. So don't ride your pony too close to others that you don't know. Never ride

right up behind another pony as it may kick yours. Warn other riders not to ride right behind your own pony for the same reason. If you meet other riders and ponies when you're out riding, always slow down to a walk, and ask if it's OK to pass. If one pony gets excited or misbehaves, wait until it's settled down before you ride past it. If you're riding on a road, keep in single file to allow plenty of room for traffic to pass you. If you get to a place where you want to canter, check with the others that they are happy for you to do so and ready to do so themselves. Never just canter off without warning, or charge past another pony and rider. If anyone seems to be getting into trouble when you are all cantering, slow down and eventually pull up to walking pace and make

sure everyone is OK before continuing. Sometimes, when a pony is used to being ridden out in a group, it may decide it doesn't want to go out on its own. It may refuse to leave the yard. It has to be taught to get over this, as a pony should be willing both to go out on its own and to go out with others. You'll find out how to cure this and other problems in the next chapter.

Riding in a
group

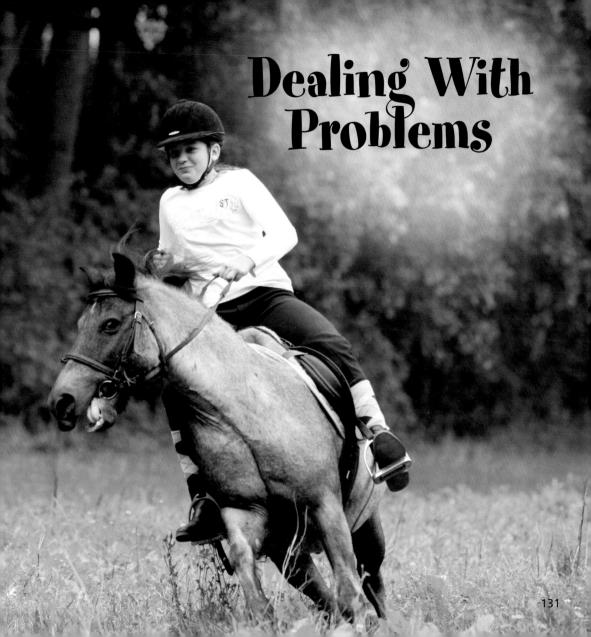

Dealing With Problems

Dealing With Problems

If your pony does not behave as you wish it to, and does not follow your instructions, before blaming it or getting mad at it stop and think about the signals you gave. Are you sure you gave the right signals? Did you give them clearly enough? If you're not sure about the answers to these questions, check what the aids should be and then try again, thinking more carefully about what you're doing.

Many instances of bad behavior are a sign that something is wrong with the pony. It may have a painful back, a sore tooth, or its tack may fit badly or be chafing. The rider may not understand the pony, and either be asking too much of it, or just giving the wrong signals. The rider may also be insufficiently experienced to cope with a particular pony. Very few ponies are difficult and aggressive by nature. When they behave badly, it is usually the result of fear, bad handling in the past, or bad experiences they have had. So if something is wrong, you need to do a little detective work. Stop and think, observe and deduce, to try to work out what the problem is and what its cause is. It's not easy, and you may need some expert help, but try hard to discover the cause of the problem before simply blaming the pony.

Here are some of the things you can do to help cure various problems.

What To Do About...

Shying

Shying is when a pony jumps sideways when confronted by something that frightens it. Shying can be caused by real fear, or occasionally by playfulness or the pony being too naughty. As we saw in the section on sight, ponies don't see things in quite the same way as we do, so something we recognize as harmless may be seen by a pony as unusual and threatening. For this reason it may shy each time it passes a certain object, even though nothing happened to upset it when it passed the object on previous occasions. We think it is being stupid, but because of changes in the light it may see the object quite differently each time, and not realize it is, in fact, the same familiar thing. Trying to force the pony past the object that frightens it can make matters worse. If possible, try walking it past several times, first from a distance of a few yards away, and gradually getting nearer each time. The pony should begin to realize that there is no real threat. Sometimes it helps to let the pony stop and look at the object for a while before coaxing it to go past. Use an encouraging tone of voice and press your legs into its sides, but don't try to force it. Or you can get off and lead the pony up to the object, letting it stop, have a good look at it, and sniff at it. Another alternative is to get a calm pony to "give you a lead" by walking past the object in front of your pony, who may well then follow without a problem.

Balking

Balking is refusing to go the way the rider wants to go. This may mean refusing to move in a certain direction, refusing to leave the yard and the pony's companions, or refusing to jump. It can be caused by fear, by being unused to going out alone and feeling nervous about it, by stubbornness and wanting to have its own way, or, in the case of jumping, by having been jumped too much and gotten tired of it, or possibly by the rider having consistently pulled its mouth on landing. If the pony sticks its toes in the ground and just won't move, you can try turning it in a tight circle, which it will dislike, so it may decide it's easier to go forwards. If it is genuinely frightened get a friend to ride a pony out ahead of yours, and the chances are that yours will follow it.

Sometimes dismounting and leading the pony will work, and once you're over the particular problem, get back on again and it may well continue without difficulty.

If the pony refuses to move at all and you think it is being naughty and willful, you could try just sitting there and not moving anywhere until it gets bored. The pony will be puzzled, and after a while it may decide it's time to go home and eat, which will prompt it to move forwards.

Balking when jumping can take the form of refusing, i.e. stopping in front of the fence, or running out, which is going sideways past the fence at the last minute instead of over it. If the pony does either of these things, ask yourself if you have been overdoing its jumping, or if you may have pulled the pony's mouth. Try taking a few days off from jumping and go out for trail rides instead. And make sure that when you start your jumping again, you keep in forward position until the pony has landed from the jump and begun to move forwards again, so you don't hurt its mouth.

Bucking

Bucking is when a pony puts its head down and kicks its heels up in the air. A pony usually bucks when it's feeling full of the joys of life and acts naughty, often when you start to canter. Bucking is usually harmless, and if you can ride well you'll be able to sit through a buck, but if the pony performs a series of bucks it can easily get you off balance and you may end up on the ground. Bucking can also be caused by a sore back, which may be the result of a saddle, girth or numnah fitting badly and chafing the pony. So if your pony bucks, you need to check first that nothing is wrong with the saddle, and that the pony hasn't been rubbed sore. Check the area that the saddle and girth cover,

and then check the underneath of the saddle, the girth, and the numnah if you use one, for lumps of mud and dried sweat. Artificial sheepskin numnahs can get caked with dried sweat, which makes them lumpy, hard and uncomfortable. Make sure the girth isn't pinching. If all seems well, and it is likely that the pony is bucking because it is just being naughty, then giving it more exercise will help. Cut down on its hard feed as well, or change it to a less energy-boosting feed.

If your pony still bucks when going into a canter, keep your reins short to keep the pony's head up, and if it really gets difficult bring it back to trot and, if necessary, walk.

Some ponies are called "cold-backed." You can recognize them by the way they dip their backs when you put on the saddle, and sometimes when you mount them. This type of pony sometimes bucks because of discomfort in its back, and if this happens get it examined by a vet. When a pony hasn't been working for some time and is likely to be too fresh (ponies that live out in a field don't usually fall into this category), it is a good idea to lunge it before riding to get rid of some of its surplus energy.

Rearing

Rearing is when a pony goes up on its hind legs, and a pony that rears when being ridden is not suitable for a young rider. Rearing can be caused by an uncomfortable bit, or by a rider that pulls on the mouth a lot. It can also be an extreme means of resisting the rider's wishes. When rearing, if a pony goes up high enough, it can overbalance and fall backwards, which is extremely dangerous as it can land on its rider. If you are ever on a pony that rears, grab hold of its mane to help you keep your balance and lean forwards to try to avoid having your weight pull it over backwards.

Running Away

A pony's natural response to danger is to run away from it as fast as it can. If a pony really panics and runs away, its fear may take over, and it forgets all its training and takes no notice at all of its rider, even if it is normally obedient. But some ponies make a habit of taking off in this manner, for no apparent reason, and they are not suitable for young and inexperienced riders. You can sometimes tell that a pony is about to do this by the way its body tenses just before it launches itself forward. If this happens, try to bring it around in a circle, which will slow it down. A pony that runs away with its rider is potentially extremely dangerous, and you shouldn't be riding it.

There is, however, a difference between a pony that makes a habit of suddenly shooting off for no apparent reason and one that is genuinely startled

by something, for example, a bird suddenly flying up very close to it, which may cause it to run off for a short distance before calming down of its own accord. Even a normally quiet pony can do that if it is sufficiently startled.

But the pony that makes a habit of galloping off for no reason at all may well have something seriously wrong with it, and should not be ridden by

young riders. Sometimes an experienced rider can re-school such a pony and cure it of its habit, but that is a job for an expert.

Pulling

There is a big difference between a pony suddenly galloping off into the distance and one that pulls. A pony that pulls your arms out, usually when you canter, generally has a hard mouth that has become deadened to feeling by heavy-handed riders. Some ponies put their heads down and lean on their bits even when trotting, which is very uncomfortable for the rider. Wearing a strong bit can cause a pony to pull. If its mouth has not been damaged by heavy handling, riding it with a more gentle bit can stop the problem. More basic schooling, encouraging the pony to obey the rider's aids with instant relaxation of the aids when it does so, can teach it not to pull. But this is a job for an experienced rider. He or she can re-school the pony to alter its balance, so its weight is less on its forehand, and it places its hind legs further

under its body and alters its center of gravity. In this position the pony will then be much less inclined to lean on the bit and to pull.

If you are riding a pony that is pulling, it's no use just setting yourself against it and pulling back, because it will always win. Look at a pony's neck – it has much larger muscles than your arms! So, what do you do? Try pulling back in short, sharp bursts, then relaxing your hands, and repeat this several times, taking your weight on your feet in the stirrups. If this doesn't work, you can try pulling hard first with one hand and then with another. This may seem brutal, but if the pony has a really hard mouth it will not hurt it, and it may help you to bring it to a halt.

Nipping and Biting
As we have seen, giving a pony too many tidbits can encourage it to nip to persuade you to give more. Prevention is always better than cure, so don't feed too many tidbits! If a pony does nip, say,

"No," very firmly. You can reinforce this with a slap on its neck if necessary. Sometimes retaliation, in the form of getting hold of its top lip with your hand and giving it a pinch of your own, can work, as the pony is taken by surprise. Keep an eye on a pony that nips, and repeat your, "No," every time you see it thinking about it.

Some ponies have an unpleasant habit of nipping or biting when you groom them or when you tighten their girths. Again, a firm, "No," can stop them, but if it doesn't, accompany the scolding

with a slap on the neck. When they stop trying to bite, praise them and change your tone of voice to sound encouraging and friendly. You can prevent them wanting to nip and bite when you tighten the girth by doing it gradually, starting by putting it on the bottom hole and then tightening it later before you mount. And you can discourage them from nipping when being groomed by using the brushes quite firmly, otherwise you may just be tickling them, and this may make them irritable.

If you do ever get seriously bitten, and the pony's teeth break through your skin and make it bleed, you may need a tetanus shot. If you are not sure whether you have had these injections in the past, or if they are not up-to-date, then see your doctor without delay.

Excitability

Some highly strung ponies become very excited in certain situations, for example, when they are with other ponies, when they are at a competition, or even

when they approach their favorite cantering spot. They tend to stick their heads in the air, to avoid the action of the bit, which makes them hollow their backs and become unbalanced. The natural tendency for the rider is to keep a firm grip on the reins in case the pony runs off, and to avoid contact with the legs, because the last thing they want to do is to send the pony forwards any faster. It probably feels as if it will leap forwards and whiz off at great speed anyway. The problem is that the pony is used to feeling contact with its rider's legs and hands, and doesn't understand the lack of leg contact. So rather than do this, it is better to ride it in small circles, using your legs lightly and keeping contact with the rein just enough to control the pony. It is easier to control the pony if it is moving in a circle. As you work the pony it should relax its neck and back, bringing its head back to the normal position. When it does so, give it a pat on the neck and say, "Good boy/girl," in an encouraging tone of voice, and relax your aids. It may take some time to re-educate the pony completely, but it is worth persevering.

Headshaking

Some ponies have an annoying habit of shaking their heads when being ridden. This is often caused by flies and gnats, as some ponies are actually allergic to their bites. Often you can cure the habit, or at any rate improve it a lot, by fitting the pony with a fly mask (see page 89) – a sort of mesh helmet that covers the pony's face and prevents the flies and gnats from biting it. These masks look strange, but ponies soon adapt to them, and seem to enjoy wearing them, as they appear to understand that they provide protection from flies.

Sometimes headshaking can be caused by ear mites, so it is a good idea to examine the ears and if they look dirty inside, treat them for mites. You can get a preparation to do this from your vet.

If the problem persists, get the pony examined by a vet, as there may be some other cause.

Stable Vices

This is a term that horsey people use to mean bad habits that horses and ponies develop when they are kept in a stable. They are usually caused by boredom and by having to live an unnatural life confined indoors. The best cure for all of them is to let the pony have a more natural life, turning it out in the paddock with companions as much as possible.

Crib-biting

This means chewing wood. Many horses and ponies chew at their stable doors, partitions, and any other wooden surfaces that may be present. Crib-biting is said to be "infectious" – if one animal does it others may well copy it. It is a bad habit, as it can wreck the stable, and it can also cause the animal's front teeth to wear down too quickly. The habit can be caused by a lack of some kind of nutrient in the diet, so check that the pony is receiving an adequate diet and has a mineralized salt block to lick. To stop the pony chewing, you can cover exposed wooden surfaces, such as the top of the stable door, with metal strips. Sometimes giving the pony a companion helps to break the habit.

Crib biting

Wind-sucking

This is a strange habit that involves a horse or pony arching its neck, usually (but not always) gripping something with its teeth at the same time, and sucking in air. It makes a grunting noise as it does so. Horses

Wind sucking

and ponies that wind-suck tend to develop thick muscles on the underside of the neck, which can look odd, as if their necks are upside down. Most can be prevented from wind-sucking by wearing a tight leather strap around the top of the neck, just below the throat, which seems to prevent them from arching their necks.

Weaving

Weaving is swinging the head and neck from side to side, taking the weight alternately on one front foot and then on the other. It is usually caused by boredom and anxiety, though a few animals do it because their feet are causing them pain. You can get special anti-weaving bars, which have V-shaped gaps in the center through which horses can stick their heads, to fit on stable doors, which stop the habit.

Let your horse work regularly, so it doesn't get bored in the stable.

Happy horses
in a tidy
stable

145

Pony Postscript

Pony Postscript

If you're crazy about ponies, you'll never stop learning about them. Here are some more fascinating facts to intrigue you.

Anatomy and Physiology

Sloping shoulders and sloping pasterns give long, low action, and this makes a comfortable riding horse or pony. Straight shoulders and upright pasterns give higher knee action and more pulling power, which is why harness horses and ponies tend to have this conformation.

Most breeds of horses and ponies have

Sloping shoulder   Straight shoulder

18 pairs of ribs, six lumbar vertebrae and 18 tail vertebrae. Arab horses have 17 pairs of ribs, five lumbar vertebrae and 16 tail vertebrae.

The horn of a pony's hoof takes about nine months to grow from the coronary band at the top to the wall of the hoof in contact with the ground at the bottom. If the coronary band is damaged, a fault appears in the hoof, which then has to grow out.

A pony's hoof is made of layers called laminae, or leaves. The inner laminae, which wrap around the bones, are sensitive. The outer laminae form the horn which encases the hoof, and are insensitive. This is why farriers can drive nails through the horn to hold on a shoe without injuring a pony.

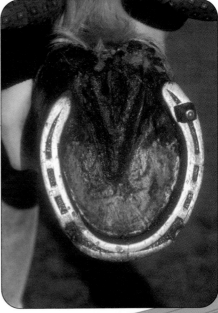

Horses and ponies have a gap between their front teeth (incisors) and back teeth (molars). This allows us to use a bit in their mouths. If they did not have this gap, we couldn't use bits on them – and the whole course of human history might have been different!

A horse's knee joint is equivalent to a person's wrist; its stifle joint is equivalent to a person's knee. The hock corresponds to a person's heel.

Horses cannot breathe through their mouths like we can. When they are breathing hard, for example, after running in a race, their nostrils dilate enormously to let them take in more air.

A horse uses a liter of oxygen a minute when it is walking; almost 60 liters a minute when galloping.

Horses use 10 percent less energy standing up than they do lying down.

When people groom horses and ponies in the areas where they "groom" each other – the neck, back and shoulders – the horses' and ponies' heart rate decreases by about 11 percent.

A horse drinks between 5 – 15 gallons (23 – 68 liters) of water a day. It drinks more water when it is stabled and fed on hay than it does if it is grazing in a paddock.

Horses exercised really hard can lose almost 10 liters of water through sweating in ten minutes.

If you work a horse or pony hard in winter, you need to clip its coat to prevent it from sweating too much. There are various different patterns of clips you can use according to how much of the coat you want to remove.

Blanket clip

Belly clip

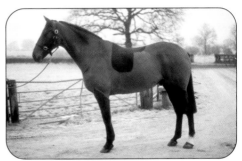

Hunter clip

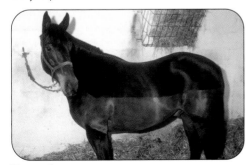

Trace clip

Low trace clip

Paces

A horse's or pony's natural paces are walk, trot, canter and gallop. It walks at about 4 mph (miles per hour – or 6.5 km/h), trots at about 7 – 8 mph (11 – 13 km/h), and canters at about 12 – 15 mph (20 – 24 km/h). The fastest racehorses can gallop at around 40 mph (65 km/h).

In both the canter and the gallop, there is a split second when all of the horse's or pony's feet are off the ground at the same time. There is also a moment when all the animal's weight is taken on one foot.

Here is Wee Bucking Willy showing the trot (left) and the canter (above) with all weight on one foot and all feet off the ground.

Some horses and ponies can move at different gaits also. The Icelandic pony, which is only 12.3 to 13.2 hh (hands high), but is always called a horse, has two special gaits, the pace, or skeid, in which pairs of legs on the same side move together, and the tölt, or running walk, which is a fast, four-beat pace.

Some American horse breeds also have special gaits. The American Standardbred, a harness racing horse, paces, or moves both legs on the same side together (like the Icelandic), as well as trots. There are trotting races and pacing races for them to compete in.

The Tennessee Walking Horse, which was bred to be ridden around plantations in the southern USA, has three special gaits: a flat walk, a running walk, and a smooth, slow canter. All are said to be very comfortable for the rider.

The American Saddlebred can be either three-gaited or five-gaited. Three-gaited horses can perform the walk, trot and canter with their legs lifted high off the ground. Five-gaited horses can also perform the "slow gait" and the rack, a very fast pace.

The Missouri Foxtrotter has an extraordinary gait in which it walks with its front legs and trots with its hing legs, its hind feet reaching well forwards and then hitting the ground with a sliding movement. At this pace it can travel at 10 mph (16 km/h).

The Peruvian Paso also paces, with the forelegs lifted high and the hind legs kept low. It is said to be a good gait for traveling over rough terrain.

Icelandic
Horses

American
Standardbred

157

Tennessee
Walking Horse

American
Saddlebred

Missouri Fox
Trotter

Peruvian
Paso

History

Xenophon, a general and historian in ancient Greece who lived from approximately 430 to 355 BC, wrote a book about riding and training horses which described procedures still used today.

Ancient breeds of pony, like the Highland and the Fjord, are dun colored, with rings of dark hair on the hocks and knees – all very like the coloring of primitive horses and ponies. Ponies shown on paintings in the caves at Lascaux, France, look very similar. These paintings are thought to date from 15,000 to 20,000 BC.

Highland Pony

Cave paintings

Norwegian
Fjord Horses

Highland
Ponies

Konik
Ponies

Horses and ponies have been shod since Roman times.

The Exmoor pony, the oldest of Britain's mountain and moorland breeds, has existed since before the last Ice Age. It has characteristic coloring, with a light, "mealy" colored ring around the eye, and the same color on the muzzle and underparts. It has no white markings at all.

The ancestry of all English Thoroughbreds can be traced back to three Arabian stallions which lived in the 17th and 18th centuries: the Darley Arabian, the Godolphin Arabian and the Byerley Turk. The Thoroughbred is the fastest breed of horse in the world.

All American Morgan horses are descended from one stallion, which lived in the late 18th century and was named Justin Morgan after his owner.

Exmoor
Ponies

English
Thoroughbred

Morgan

Show jumping was first included in the Olympic Games in 1900 in Paris.

Eventing, which comprises dressage, cross-country and show jumping, was originally called combined training. It was developed mostly by military riders.

Pictures from Junior Jumping and Cross Country at Hickstead, UK.

Eventing –
Cross Country

171

Horsey terms

An "easy keeper" is a horse or pony that manages to look well fed and sleek on small amounts of food. This type of animal tends to have a calm and relaxed outlook on life, and can very easily get too fat.

A "hard keeper" is the opposite – an animal that, no matter how well it is fed, tends to be on the thin side. Hard keepers tend to be nervy and neurotic. When returning from exercise they can break out into a sweat in their stables, become agitated, and refuse to eat.

A horse or pony is said to be "sound" when it is healthy, and has no lameness or breathing problems.

"Breaking" a horse or pony, in horsey language, has nothing to do with leg casts! It means the first time a horse or pony is ridden, when it is being "broken in."

When a horse or pony is said to have "good bone," it refers to the measurement around the forelegs, just below the knee. When this measurement is high, the animal has strong legs and is capable of carrying a heavy rider.

"Going" is the condition of the ground when it is used for riding activities. "Heavy going" means the ground is muddy, soft and wet; "hard going" means it is dry and hard. "Good going" is in between, soft enough to ride on but not too soft.

When a horse's or pony's head is held in the position in which the rider has the maximum control over it (when it is held vertically to the ground) it is said to be "on the bit."

The left-hand side of a horse or pony is called the "nearside."

The right-hand side of a horse or pony is called the "offside."

On the bit

The front part of a horse or pony – head, neck, shoulders and forelegs – is called the "forehand."

"Impulsion" is a difficult word to understand. It means the energy a rider creates in a horse or pony by the use of his or her legs and seat, which gives the animal its driving force to move forwards.

"Outline" means the shape a horse's or pony's body makes when it is being ridden.

"Collection" means moving with shorter, higher strides, which shortens the horse's outline. "Extension" means moving with longer, lower strides, which lengthens the horse's outline.

Notes

Notes

Welsh
Section D

Konik Ponies

Gypsy Vanner
Horses

Fell Ponies